USA TODAY bestselling author **Janice Maynard** loved books and writing even as a child. After multiple rejections, she finally sold her first manuscript! Since then, she has written sixty books and novellas. Janice lives in Tennessee with her husband, Charles. They love hiking, travelling and family time. You can connect with Janice at

www.janicemaynard.com, www.Twitter.com/janicemaynard, www.Facebook.com/janicemaynardauthor, www.Facebook.com/janicesmaynard and www.Instagram.com/therealjanicemaynard.

An Heir
of His Own

JANICE
MAYNARD

MILLS & BOON

First published in Great Britain 2021
by Mills & Boon, an imprint of HarperCollins*Publishers* Ltd,
1 London Bridge Street, London, SE1 9GF

www.harpercollins.co.uk

HarperCollins*Publishers*
1st Floor, Watermarque Building,
Ringsend Road, Dublin 4, Ireland

Large Print edition 2021

An Heir of His Own © 2021 Harlequin Books S.A.

Special thanks and acknowledgement are given to
Janice Maynard for her contribution to the
Texas Cattleman's Club: Fathers and Sons miniseries.

ISBN: 978-0-263-29326-5

11/21

MIX
Paper from
responsible sources
FSC C007454

For all the health-care workers
who have sustained us.
Thank you for your dedication!

One

Cammie Wentworth exited Royal Memorial Hospital via the heavy plate-glass doors and paused on the front walk, exhaling in relief and breathing in the delicious October air. Her favorite month of the year was rapidly becoming her favorite month *ever*. Hard work and single-mindedness were finally paying off.

At twenty-eight, it was about time she found her place in the world. Anticipating the meeting she had just attended with hospital administrators and influential doctors had given her several sleepless nights the past week. She worried they might think she was too young or too inexperienced. After all, her father had created a brand-new charitable foundation and made his only daughter the director.

Some people frowned on nepotism. But in this case—maybe because her father was about to drop a ton of money for a very good cause—the top brass at Royal Memorial had been open and enthusiastic about Cammie's pitch. She was determined to keep them involved and excited.

Being goal-oriented was good in the business world, but unfortunately, her more personal issues were harder to check off the list:

1) Persuade her long-lost brother, Rafe, to come home

2) Explore artificial insemination or adoption and become a mom

3) Erase every memory of Drake Rhodes and his piercing blue eyes

She was working on the first two. A few glimpses of hope kept her going. But that last one was frustratingly impossible. Even after two years, her breakup with Drake felt raw. Thankfully, he was working on the other side of the world for six months in Sydney, Australia. As far as Cammie was concerned, she hoped rabid kangaroos hopped out of the bush and ate him alive.

The bloodthirsty image made her smile again.

Drake was old history. They wanted different things.

Adjusting her shoulder bag, she turned toward the parking lot and ran smack into a hard wall of a man. When she stumbled, warm hands grabbed her shoulders and steadied her. "Sorry," he said. And then they both took a good look at the other. Cammie's shock was astounding.

"Drake?" She shook her head, wondering if the stress of this hospital meeting had tipped her over the edge. "What are you doing here?"

He was as gorgeous as ever, lanky and lean with thick, black hair and a slight swagger in his stance. Her stomach pitched and took a nosedive. Had she conjured him out of her imagination? But no, he was distressingly real.

Her heart, which she had thought mostly healed, cracked again.

* * *

Drake Rhodes was shocked as hell and trying not to let on. Surely fate was testing him. He'd barely been back in Royal for a nanosecond, and already he'd run into Cammie? He couldn't decide if he was angry or excited or both.

"Hello, Cam." Cammie Wentworth was stunning in the unforgiving midday sun. Her skin had the pale translucence of a true redhead, and her long, wavy hair gleamed with highlights of gold. He remembered making love to every inch of her tall, gently curved body.

Green eyes stared at him with suspicion. "I asked you a question."

He shook his head to clear the cobwebs and the memories trapped there. "Ainsley suffered a ruptured appendix."

"Oh, no."

"She's going to be okay, thank goodness. My stepsister has a long history of disrupting my life." He said that last bit with a grin. Cammie knew the story—how Drake had offered to be Ainsley's guardian when she was orphaned seven years ago. Ainsley had been fifteen, Drake only twenty-two. "I was just headed upstairs to see her," he said.

Cammie's face closed up. "Well, I won't keep you."

Drake noticed that she didn't say *nice to see you* or *how have you been?* Cammie wasn't a fan of his—for reasons that were entirely understandable. Even so, the lukewarm response depressed him.

He took her arm. "I'll walk you to your car, and maybe you can tell me why you're here."

Cammie gave him a tight-lipped stare, shaking off his light hold. "It's broad daylight. Ainsley will be waiting for you. I don't need an escort."

"Humor me." He didn't know why he was pushing. But this might be his only chance to reconnect with Cammie and to see if she had gotten past his cruel rejection.

Cammie's halting confession two years ago about wanting a baby had been like a dash of cold water in his face. What if a condom broke? What if other birth control failed? The thought of having to raise another child scared the crap out of him. Ainsley had required enough parenting for a lifetime. Thank God she was an adult now. He was off the hook.

And yet something in him was glad to see Cammie again.

His ex-girlfriend was clearly trying to ignore him, because she walked quickly—two steps ahead—through the jammed parking lot. Suddenly, she stopped. "I swear, this place is a maze. I thought I parked on this row."

"That big pickup truck at the end is blocking your view. Why don't you try beeping your key fob?"

Cammie grimaced. "Whatever would I do without a big strong man to give me advice?" She pointed and beeped. Yep, they were in the right place. As they rounded the bumper of the obligatory Texas-male vehicle, two things happened at once—Drake heard the unmistakable sound of a baby crying, and he saw something on Cammie's trunk.

Not *something*. A someone. A very unhappy baby strapped into a small car seat. "What the hell?"

Cammie approached her car warily, looking

from side to side. "Is this a practical joke?" They scanned the area for the child's mother or father.

Drake frowned, his protective instincts on high alert. "More like the beginnings of a scam. I've heard about situations like this. Somebody shows up asking for money. Or accusing you of kidnapping." Maybe this was why he had insisted on following her. Maybe he was in the right place at the right time.

Cammie wanted a baby badly. She had seriously thought about the prospect for at least the past five years.

But she hadn't expected one to drop out of the sky. This was just plain weird.

She approached the car and the kid cautiously. The baby screamed louder. Even for a woman with strong maternal instincts, the volume began to make her panic. But she sure as heck wasn't going to let Drake see that she was flustered.

She shot him a look. "I'm serious," she said. "You should go." Quickly, she unlocked her car and tossed her bag on the front seat. Since she had been inside a hospital moments ago, she grabbed sanitizer and cleaned her hands. Then she reached out and began unfastening and loosening all the buckles and straps keeping the infant safe.

Drake stood far too close, his gaze cataloging her every move. "I don't think you should pick it up. There are liability issues."

"Not an *it*," she said. "A baby."

"I can see that…"

The little body was warm. Its face was red. She glanced sideways to see Drake pull his phone from his pocket. "What are you doing?"

He lifted an eyebrow as if questioning her intelligence. "Calling 911?"

"Oh, right. Sorry, I'm a little rattled."

"That makes two of us."

Cammie guessed the baby was a boy. The one-piece pajamas he wore were blue-and-white plaid. A matching cap protected his small head. "Hey, there, munchkin," she whispered, hoping her presence would soothe him. As she scooped him out of his cocoon, she kept up a steady stream of soft, reassuring words. "You're beautiful, did you know that? It's okay for boys to be beautiful, I promise."

Drake snorted but didn't say anything. He was on his phone waiting for an answer.

Cammie cradled the infant against her breast, relieved when the shrieking cries subsided into whimpers. He was warm and solid in her arms. It was impossible to know for sure, but she guessed the child was a month old, maybe six weeks. He had black eyes and black wispy curls. His gaze seemed to lock on to hers, but that might be her imagination.

Whenever she imagined having a baby one day, the baby always looked like Drake. *Dumb, Cammie. Really dumb...*

Now that the immediate crisis was over, she knew she had a very short time to find his family. Babies as young as this one liked to eat often. There was no diaper bag, no note with instructions, nothing. The sheer impossibility of the situation made her think, once again, that someone was pranking her. If so, the joke was in very poor taste.

Fortunately, Drake's phone call bore fruit. The 911 operator was professional and didn't waste any time. With the call complete, Cammie leaned against the car and waited. Drake stood, aloof and quiet. If it had been hotter,

Cammie would have sheltered inside the vehicle with the air-conditioning running. Fortunately, the weather was delightful.

Now that the infant had stopped crying, she was able to concentrate on his unmistakable appeal. The tiny boy smelled of baby lotion and all those other wonderful aromas that were part of the package with a newborn. Keeping her attention on the boy made it possible for her to *appear* to ignore Drake.

Finally, she turned to face the man who had broken her heart. "You need to go now. I've got this."

Drake's posture and his level gaze were stoic. "I'm not leaving you."

Unfortunately, the baby was getting squirmy and fussy. Cammie put him on her shoulder, cradled his head and tried walking back and forth. Maybe the warmth of her body and the motion would reassure him. Even so, an empty stomach was not going to be so easily appeased.

Fortunately, the police arrived quickly.

The officer who stepped out of the patrol car was female—a tall, slender Latina with long dark hair and dark eyes. In fact, she could easily have been the child's mother.

Cammie clutched the baby tighter. "Thanks for coming," she said. "My name is Cammie Wentworth. This is Drake Rhodes. We didn't know what else to do but call the police."

"I'm Haley Lopez. Tell me what happened."

The story was short and sweet. Cammie related everything she knew. "I'm afraid he'll be getting hungry any second." Drake didn't interrupt, but he stood close by, his gaze concerned.

Haley nodded. "No worries. I'll line up social services in a jiffy." She moved a few strides away to deal with the call.

While Officer Lopez was on the phone, a second woman stepped out of the cruiser. No badge this time, but she had some sort of credentials hanging around her neck. "Hey," she said. "I'm Sierra Morgan. I've been doing a ride-along with Officer Lopez, hoping to get acquainted with some of Maverick County." Sierra was petite, with long blond hair and green eyes. "I heard something about a baby?"

"He's not mine," Cammie said. "I found him

on my car. Have you had a busy morning out on the mean streets of Royal?"

Sierra smiled ruefully, including Drake in her gaze. "Let's just say that an abandoned baby is the most interesting thing we've come across all day."

Drake spoke up. "Are you an aspiring police officer?"

"Oh, heck no," Sierra said. "I'm a journalist for *America* magazine." She pointed at the credentials draped around her neck. "I'm here in Royal to do an article on the upcoming gala and the tenth anniversary of the Texas Cattleman's Club finally admitting women." She wrinkled her nose. "Seriously? Only ten years? That's pretty sad."

Drake nodded wryly. "Change happens slowly around here. If you stay long enough, you'll see what I mean."

Cammie wasn't Drake's girlfriend anymore, but she couldn't deny the curl of jealousy in her stomach. Drake and Sierra were hitting it off a little too well.

Sierra turned back to Cammie. "Here's my business card. You never know—I might end up doing a piece about this little sweetheart."

Cammie took the card reluctantly. *America* was a nationally recognized publication. In a day when magazines were going the way of the dodo bird, *America* was still widely available in print. Nevertheless, Cammie didn't want the baby to be the subject of some gossipy news story. How would Sierra sell it, anyway? No one but local people would be interested.

"Thanks," she said. "But I'm sure there's not much of a tale."

"You never know."

The officer finished her call and returned. She addressed Cammie and Drake. "Sorry. That took longer than I expected. There's been a multicar pileup out on the interstate. If you'll give me a moment to get the car seat in my patrol car, this little boy and I will be on our way." She paused, an odd look on her face. "May I hold him a minute? I love babies."

Cammie handed over her charge reluctantly. "Do you have any of your own?"

Officer Lopez shook her head, staring down at the little boy with a wistful expression. "No, but I do have a few nieces and nephews."

Once Cammie had the baby back in her arms, the officer made a second call to what sounded like the station, updating someone on her situation and whereabouts. Cammie wanted to ask more questions about the social services procedure. She clutched the baby tightly, disconcerted that everything was moving so quickly.

Drake could see that Cammie was uneasy. Two years ago, she'd told him she wanted a baby, but this wasn't it. Besides, he still had a bad feeling about the entire bizarre encounter. Until he had evidence to the contrary, he would assume Cammie needed backup.

He watched her take a deep breath, not looking at him or at the reporter, but at Haley Lopez. "I want to keep him," she said. "Until his mother or father is found."

The officer shook her head. "Sorry. We have a protocol to follow. We utilize foster parents who are certified. I can't just hand him over."

Cammie was pale, almost teary-eyed. "Don't they say possession is nine-tenths of the law?"

Drake felt odd emotions in his chest. Regret. Confusion, Incredulity. First Ainsley, now this.

The universe was clearly offering him a chance to make up for his sins. And the little devil whispering in his ear pointed out how nice it would be to have Cammie close.

He cleared his throat. "Officer Lopez, I'm a licensed foster parent in the state of Texas. I had to jump through the hoops when I took over the care of my stepsister, Ainsley, seven years ago. If Ms. Wentworth is willing, I can go on record as being the kid's foster parent." He shot Cammie a pointed look. "But Ms. Wentworth will have to move into my house and actually care for the child."

Officer Lopez raised her eyebrows. "That seems a lot to ask."

Cammie glared at Drake. "Mr. Rhodes and I know each other." Her eyes were wide, her gaze hunted as she assessed his offer. She chewed her bottom lip, clearly debating her options. "You don't even live here right now, Drake. How would this work?"

He addressed the three women equally, keeping his expression impassive. "My stepsister suffered a ruptured appendix. I've come back to Royal to make sure she's okay. As Cammie knows, the house Ainsley lives in belongs to me. Cammie and the baby are welcome to stay. Ainsley will be in the hospital for several more days. When she is completely back to normal, I'll be returning to Australia. But by then, I'm sure the child's parents will have been located."

Haley Lopez nodded. "I think that can work. I'll need some information from you, Mr. Rhodes. Do you mind stepping over to the cruiser? I'll run your credentials and make sure I have the all clear."

As Drake followed the officer to her car, he kept an eye on Cammie. Her entire attention was focused on the baby. Seeing her again ripped at the scabbed-over guilt he carried. He knew he had hurt her. But what else could he have done? The two of them were polar opposites.

Cammie was soft and maternal and caring. Drake was…well, not that.

There was an old '70s song his mother used to sing. Something about being cruel to be kind. That summed up his broken relationship with Cammie perfectly.

Here was his chance to soften the edges of that pesky guilt. By helping Cammie in this situation, he could absolve himself and hopefully make her happy.

The danger was, he might hurt her again. Equally bad would be to remember how much he had wanted her, even when he broke off the relationship.

Could he keep himself in line? Could he resist the urge to get sucked back into Cammie's orbit of hearth and home?

He never wanted kids. Which meant he couldn't have Cammie.

Being close to her again would be torture.

He gave the officer his Social Security number and birth date and waited while she entered his info and spoke with social services. Soon, the deed was done.

When he and Lopez approached Cammie, she looked up with naked hope on her face. In the past, Drake had been a pro at squashing that kind of hope. But not this time.

Seeing her with a baby in her arms squeezed his heart. This was what Cammie wanted.

Though it seemed risky as hell, Drake was going to pay for his sins with a short-term experiment. For once, he would even the scales and make Cammie happy. He owed her this much at least. His libido was all in favor of the tantalizing idea—Drake and Cammie under one roof.

Haley Lopez smiled at Cammie. "Are you sure about this, Ms. Wentworth? Newborns demand an incredible amount of work."

Cammie squared her shoulders. "I want to do it. *Somebody* put this baby on my car. That gives me an odd sort of responsibility. Plus, it will only be for a short time, surely."

The officer nodded. "I think you're right. But don't get too attached. I've seen foster parents grieve."

"I know he's not mine," Cammie said.

Drake touched the child's hair briefly, charmed in spite of himself. "What will you call him? I doubt he'll answer to *hey, you*."

Cammie actually laughed, her green eyes clear and bright when her gaze met his. "Well," she said. "It *is* October. What if I call him Pumpkin?"

Haley Lopez smiled. "I like it."

Cammie shot Drake a challenging glance. "What do *you* think?"

He shoved his hands in his pockets. The urge to touch the baby again was alarming. "Whatever," he said, shrugging to prove that he didn't care one way or another.

And just like that, Cammie's beautiful smile faded.

She turned to the officer. "Am I free to go? I'll give you one of my business cards."

Haley Lopez nodded. "I think you *should* go. As quickly as possible. There's a combo market/pharmacy on the other side of the hospital. They sell premixed formula. It's super expensive, but in this situation, I doubt you have much time." She looked at Drake. "Will you help her get home and settled?"

He fished a key ring out of his pocket and handed one key to Cammie. "Here's a spare. Make yourself comfortable. Mrs. Hampton was there this morning." To Haley, he said, "My housekeeper splits her time between taking care of the house and my ranch on the outskirts of town." Turning back to Cammie, he continued, "Ainsley's bedroom is upstairs. You and the baby are welcome to the guest bedroom on the main floor."

Why did he feel the need to explain why he wasn't going with her? Cammie was the one who wanted to play with the baby. Not him. When neither woman said a word, he shrugged. "I have to go see my stepsister right now. She's expecting me. What if I pick up some food on the way home?"

Officer Lopez nodded. "Divide and conquer. Sounds like a plan."

Drake rubbed the back of his neck, wondering why Cammie's blank expression made him feel like crap. "Text me if you need anything, Cammie. The number is the same. I have a different phone in Australia."

"I'm sure the baby and I will be fine. I appreciate your making this happen."

If her words had been any stiffer, they would have shattered like glass.

Drake felt a tension headache brewing. Was he making a terrible mistake? Was he going to get burned again? It didn't really matter, because he owed her. "I'll see you later," he muttered. Then he strode toward the hospital.

* * *

Cammie was heartsick as she watched Drake walk away. Intellectually, she understood that he had to see his stepsister, but despite the truth of the matter, she felt abandoned again. Some stupid part of her wanted Drake to be as excited about the baby as she was.

After the car seat was anchored in her car, she memorized the steps as she watched the officer secure the baby. Haley pointed to the chest strap. "You'll want to loosen this before you get him out."

"Got it," Cammie said, her throat dry. She was tempted to *walk* to the market. It wasn't that far. But the car would be faster, and she was positive it was time for the baby to eat. His little face turned red as he whimpered.

In the store, she didn't waste any time looking for what she needed. She went straight to an employee and asked for assistance.

The woman was super helpful. "These bottles of formula are ready to go. You simply pop off the plastic cap, and the nipples are already sterile."

Thank God. Cammie paid for two six-packs,

along with diapers and wipes and new pj's, because that was all she could carry. At the same time, she arranged to have more items delivered to Drake's house the following morning. An infant couldn't demolish more than twelve of these bottles overnight. Or so she hoped.

Back at the car, she turned on the AC and moved her seat back as far as it would go. With the baby cradled in her left arm, she popped open one of the bottles and nudged the nipple against his lips. To her eternal relief, the kid opened his mouth and began sucking greedily.

Though the baby occupied her attention, other thoughts raced in her brain. Drake was back in Royal. He wasn't in Australia. An odd mix of joy and trepidation squeezed her heart. He had offered to let her stay with him.

It was a tiny miracle. Either that or a disaster waiting to happen. She was over him. Wasn't she?

Then how did she explain the excitement fizzing in her veins?

After two ounces, she lifted the baby to her shoulder and was gratified to get a healthy burp. With it came a shot of spit-up on her navy suit jacket. Lesson learned. She was going to need burp cloths.

The little boy went right back to eating when she offered the formula a second time. The bottle wasn't quite empty when his eyes closed, and he conked out.

Cammie sat there holding him, knowing she had dodged a bullet. What if he had been allergic? What if he was normally breastfed and wouldn't take a bottle?

It didn't take a shrink to see that she was focusing on the baby so she wouldn't have to think about returning to Drake's house. By the time she arrived at the very familiar address, she was exhausted.

Although she had spent plenty of time there in the past, none of it had been in the guest room. She had shared Drake's large, hedonistic bed. The memories made her hot and restless. Laying the baby on the mattress momentarily, she kicked off her shoes and shrugged out of her stained jacket. The silk blouse underneath was sleeveless, so she immediately felt cooler.

Even the guest room had a king-size bed.

If she lined the far edge with pillows, she could throw back the covers and let the baby sleep beside her tonight. It wasn't ideal, but until she could get something more suitable ordered, it was the best she could do.

She sank down in a chair, her legs suddenly weak and shaky. Was she out of her mind? She didn't know how to take care of a baby.

The memory of Drake's deep blue eyes as he offered to be the foster parent on record confused her. Why had he done it? They had barely seen each other in two years, and then only at public functions where they both managed to stay on opposite sides of the room. The pain of their breakup had tormented her.

As for Drake...who knew? He was an enigma wrapped in a question. Kind and thoughtful one minute, remote the next.

In the midst of her soul searching, the baby slept peacefully. Where was his mother? His father? Was there a sixteen-year-old girl somewhere who simply couldn't handle motherhood? Cammie was almost thirty, but she was still scared. This brief experiment might dissuade her from becoming a single mother. No matter how badly she wanted a baby of her own, she might discover that solo parenting wasn't for her.

Because the little boy slept deeply, Cammie decided this was the time to make one of her famous to-do lists. It was going to be a doozy. She needed clothes and toiletries from her own house. Plus, her computer. Then, of course, she had to buy something for the child to sleep in. A bassinet would be fine for the short term. Pumpkin was small enough that he didn't roll over.

The clothes and blankets and pacifiers would be fun to choose online. Unless pacifiers were a no-no. She would have to research that.

Although money was not really a problem, it would make more sense to order powdered formula and learn how to mix it. On the other hand, this was a temporary situation, so maybe to preserve her sanity, the premixed formula was a worthwhile expense.

Even in the midst of her very practical thoughts, other, more incendiary considerations intruded. *Drake Rhodes.* Sleeping just down the hall from her. In the past, they hadn't been able to keep their hands off each other. To say they were sexually compatible was like calling the ocean wet. Drake was a master at giving pleasure, and she did the same for him.

Over the course of an eighteen-month sexual relationship, they had been as close as two people can be. But Cammie had been the one to cause a rift. Innocently enough. One rainy, early-autumn night, when the weather outside had been dreadful, Drake had built a fire in the fireplace. They'd ordered in, enjoyed an intimate dinner and then made love in front of the crackling flames.

They had talked afterward, wrapped in each other's arms on the lushly carpeted floor, swathed in an expensive cashmere afghan. Drake had opened up about his dreams for expanding his financial consulting business…his yearning to travel the world. He had an incredible business mind, and his investing expertise was in high demand.

Cammie had listened, and when he asked *her* a question in return, she'd been honest. She told him that she had always dreamed of becoming a mother. That she wanted a family. Roots. Her own formative years had been turbulent, to say the least, which was why she was drawn to the idea of normalcy.

On that long-ago evening, Drake hadn't said much about her revelation, but gradually over the weeks that followed, she'd felt him drawing away. He'd been busier suddenly. He had traveled more.

Because it happened so slowly, Cammie hadn't connected the dots. She had sensed that things weren't the same between them, but she didn't know why. Until the day he sat her down and told her that he didn't want to get married or have kids.

His words had been gentle, but the pain was no less traumatic. Cammie had fled this very house and never looked back.

Now she was here again. With a baby. Playing at what she had always wanted. This was probably the worst idea she had ever conceived, but she was committed now. And she was too smart to let Drake Rhodes hurt her again.

Two

Three hours after Cammie walked through Drake's front door, she was still nervously awaiting his arrival. What was taking him so long? Was he avoiding her?

She and the baby had come to an understanding. He would tolerate Cammie's clumsiness, and she would protect him from all harm. A couple of times, Cammie could swear he smiled at her. Was that possible? Did babies so young know how to smile? She told herself he did.

At four o'clock, still no Drake. Maybe he wasn't going to come home at all. Maybe he was already regretting his offer to help.

Maybe he'd decided to sleep out at his ranch. She told herself a mature woman didn't get her feelings hurt over something so unimportant, but she knew the truth.

Part of her had hoped Drake would enjoy having Pumpkin here for a temporary visit... that the man so opposed to fatherhood would see how sweet it was to have a newborn. She should be embarrassed at her own blind naïveté.

When Pumpkin was ready for another bottle, Cammie felt more confident this time. Soon, his tiny eyelashes fanned his cheeks again. She held him for a few minutes but finally put him down. He needed to sleep on his own.

When her stomach growled, she glanced at her watch. Only then did she realize she had skipped lunch. Drake had promised to bring food, but he hadn't said which meal. Surely, he hadn't stayed all this time at the hospital with Ainsley. There were rules about visiting hours. On the other hand, she knew full well that Drake enjoyed breaking rules.

A shiver snaked its way down her spine. Without the baby to distract her, she was jumpy. For two years she had kept her distance from Drake. Now she was back in his sphere. Too close. Too tempted. Memories washed over her, both exhilarating and painful.

It was her own fault. She could have handed the baby over to Officer Lopez and walked away. But something about the abandoned infant made her determined to keep him in the short term. He wasn't hers. She wasn't delusional.

Even so, she felt responsible.

When she heard the front door open just before five, her heartbeat quickened. Drake was home. Apparently, he wasn't alone, because she heard male voices. Footsteps tromped down the hall. Her host appeared in the doorway.

"Hey," he said.

That single word dried her throat. "Hello."

Drake motioned for the two college-aged kids behind him to enter the room. They carried a large box. Drake looked at Cammie. "I got a bed. I thought that wall over there might work. Is that okay?" His gaze landed briefly on the baby, who slept peacefully.

Her eyebrows shot up as she read the name on the box. It was a high-end Swedish company that made baby furniture. "Drake. Good grief. We'll probably only have Pumpkin for a few days." This one item must have cost $3,000 or more.

Drake shrugged, his expression hard to read. "Doesn't matter. We can donate it when he's gone. Excuse me. I have to answer a few emails. Give me a yell if there's a problem."

Cammie tidied the room while she watched the two pleasant and competent young men assemble the bed. The blond boards were pale and beautiful, buffed to a pleasing sheen. One of the guys smiled at her. "You've got a beauty here. This particular wood is supposed to be so hard that it barely shows teeth marks."

She wanted to laugh. Poor little Pumpkin was months away from having teeth. "I guess I'll have to choose bedding worthy of such a gorgeous heirloom."

The other workman looked up from tightening a screw on the railing. "Mr. Rhodes already took care of that. We have several more boxes out in the truck. Almost done here. Then we'll bring in the rest."

Cammie's heart sank. She didn't want to be beholden to Drake. Not like this. Was he somehow trying to buy her forgiveness? He'd been nothing but honest with her. It wasn't his fault that she wanted something he couldn't or wouldn't give her.

When the rest of Drake's exorbitantly expensive shopping spree arrived inside, Cammie didn't know whether to laugh or be scandalized. There was a mattress and sheets, a wall hanging and a baby monitor. A rocker in the same wood as the bed came with a lumbar cushion for Mom or Dad. The bed was the type that could convert for a toddler, so Drake had purchased the matching comforter and blanket and pillow.

By the time everything was in place, Pumpkin's new nest was complete, and Cammie was left to wonder where she was going to put all the rest.

At last, Drake returned. He surveyed the new items in his guest room and gave a half nod, the only signal of his approval. "Is he still sleeping?"

Cammie tried a smile, but it felt false. "Yes. But I don't know for how long."

"I had them charge the monitor to a hundred percent in the store before I left. If you can figure out how to work it, we can eat."

"You have food?" she asked, her stomach growling audibly.

For the first time, Drake's expression lightened. "I called Amanda Battle at the diner. She promised to include all your favorites. Pot roast. Mashed potatoes. Her famous broccoli salad. Hot rolls."

"And strawberry pie?"

"And strawberry pie."

He seemed uneasy, being so close to all the baby paraphernalia. "They just delivered the meal. Meet me in the kitchen when you're ready," he said brusquely. "I'll keep it warm."

And then he disappeared again.

Cammie glanced at the baby. He was sleeping on his back. She knew that much was correct. And his little face was serene. "Will you snooze long enough for me to eat dinner?" she asked.

The infant didn't answer.

Unfortunately, Cammie used precious minutes trying to figure out the monitor. But at last, she set the base on the bedside table and tiptoed out of the room carrying the little screen that allowed her to keep a watchful eye on her new responsibility.

She found Drake in the kitchen, as promised. He had shed his expensive sport coat and rolled up the sleeves of his crisp white dress shirt. She saw his tie crumpled on one of the bar stools. Even for a simple hospital visit, he dressed like the successful man he was. His muscular, tanned arms were incredibly sexy. Or maybe that was sexual deprivation talking.

It shouldn't have been a turn-on to watch a man unload a basket of food containers, but Cammie focused on Drake's every move.

He mistook her fascination for starvation. "Grab a plate," he said. "I've set us two places in the dining room."

The kitchen nook had a perfectly serviceable table, though small. Perhaps Drake thought the ambience was too cozy. By the time Cammie had served her plate, he had poured two glasses of wine and carried them into the adjoining room.

Since Cammie knew Drake's housekeeper kept the dining room table set for four all the time, she couldn't be flattered. Even the lit candles were not a nod to romance. Drake entertained often. Clearly, the candlelight was more *sophisticated mood* than a seductive prelude.

He soon joined her with his own plate. For a few awkward minutes, neither of them said a word. Cammie ate too quickly. She'd been almost light-headed with hunger. The stress of the day and the fact that she was probably a little dehydrated made the meal all the more appealing.

When she had cleared half her plate, she looked up to find Drake staring at her. A muscle ticked in his throat. "I should have brought you lunch. I'm sorry."

"Am I making a pig of myself?" She felt the hot flush that crept from her throat to her cheeks.

His gaze darkened to the deep navy of a nighttime sea. "Not at all. You always did have strong appetites."

"Don't do that," she said sharply.

His faux-innocent expression wasn't the least bit convincing. "Do what?"

"Don't bring up sex. That's not why I'm here."

His lips pressed tightly together, rolling inward, his gaze stormy. "I know that, Camellia. You've found another man."

Using her much-hated full name was his way of baiting her. But she refused to play that game. First, she needed to get something out of the way. "Thank you," she said tersely. "For all the baby stuff. It wasn't necessary. In fact, it's ridiculously over-the-top. But I do appreciate it. Pumpkin has everything he needs."

"And what about you, Cammie?" Drake's fingers toyed with a spoon on the table. "Do you have what you need?"

She pretended to misunderstand his innuendo. "I'll have to run home and pack a bag. Maybe after the next feeding. I won't be gone a whole hour. He'll sleep that long."

Her host paled. "Oh, hell no. Make a list. I know my way around your condo. You're not leaving me here alone with that kid."

"He's not that scary. Newborns sleep a lot."

"Doesn't matter. This was your gig. I'm happy to play support team."

"Fine," she said grumpily. The idea of Drake poking around her bedroom now that they were no longer lovers made her uncomfortable. But it appeared she had no choice.

After a few false starts, they finally began a conversation that was impersonal and non-threatening. She asked Drake what it was like to visit Australia. And then questioned him about the booming movie industry in Australia, because she had read an interesting news story in that vein lately. Later, he said he'd heard about her father's loss...offered his sympathy.

"Thanks," Cammie said. "It's been a hard time for him. Danae was the love of his life."

"Third time's a charm?"

"I suppose. He was crushed when her cancer was diagnosed. And honestly, he did a complete 180 in terms of his outlook. Danae wanted him to be more generous, less of a workaholic. She urged him to give back to the community, convinced him it was the road to happiness. And she begged him to reconcile with Rafe."

"Is Rafe open to that idea?"

"It doesn't seem so. I've sent letters and called him a dozen times over the years. Usually, he never answers me. Once, he simply told me he doesn't believe in looking back. Daddy has written him this time, though, so I'm hopeful."

"Wow. I never thought your dad would do that."

"Danae changed him."

"How is *your* mom?"

Cammie shrugged. "We're still not close. I see her a couple of times a year in New York, but she will never come back to Royal. I think she resents the fact that I wanted to stay here instead of going with her. But I was a kid. Royal was all I knew."

Drake was silent for a moment, his dinner finished. At last, he sighed. "I figured out something when we broke up."

She stiffened. "What do you mean?"

"I never could understand why the baby thing was such a huge deal to you, but I finally understood. It's because your relatives were and are so screwed up. You thought a baby would give you a fresh start. A tabula rasa. You wanted a do-over, a chance to create the perfect family. Am I right?"

The bite of potatoes she'd swallowed turned to a lump in her throat. After a reckless swig of wine, she managed to face him. "Wanting children is a completely normal human emotion. Otherwise, the population would die out."

"I never said it wasn't normal. But you might be trying to get pregnant for the wrong reasons."

She tamped down her fury. "I didn't know you had taken a side gig as a therapist. You don't know me well enough to understand my motivations."

His gaze narrowed. "I knew you pretty damn well once upon a time."

"Maybe."

"Admit it, Cammie. We were a perfect match until you started listening to some mythical body clock."

"We weren't a perfect match," she hissed. "You were an egotistical, self-centered, arrogant jerk, and I didn't see you for who you were until it was too late."

"So the blame is all mine?"

He was angry, too. They had summoned a whirlwind of feelings that should have dissipated by now. The past was the past.

Apparently, Drake was no more sanguine about their breakup than she was.

She took a deep breath, counted to ten. "This isn't a productive conversation. If you won't let me leave you with the baby for a short time, then I'll make a list of what I need. I'll give you my key."

"I still have one," he said curtly, his expression impossible to read.

Her mouth dropped open. Those four words shocked her. She wanted to ask him why, but she didn't want to hear his answer. Perhaps the more important question was, why had *she* never asked him to return her key?

To say they had both forgotten seemed naive in the extreme.

Her stomach tightened with tension. "Pumpkin will be awake soon. I'll go make a list. Will you be in your office?"

"There or the den. You can find me. You know your way around."

He was still trying to provoke her. Instead of responding, she walked out of the room.

* * *

Drake took his time driving to Cammie's place. He was angry and frustrated, and he didn't enjoy either emotion. Already, he regretted his impulsive invitation. Having Cammie and the baby in his house was sure to drive him insane.

Maybe he was a glutton for punishment.

Walking through the front door of Cammie's modern, spacious condo had him drowning in emotions. Lust was the big one, but so many more. He could see himself here, vividly. All the nights she had cooked for him. All the relaxed weekend mornings they'd lazed in her bed and made love again and again.

When his body tightened and his sex inevitably stirred, he cursed beneath his breath. He had moved on. So had Cammie. It was for the best.

He pulled open the door of her walk-in closet and was assailed by her scent. Once upon a time, he had tried to buy her perfume, but she told him she preferred simpler fragrances. Lemon. Lavender.

In the midst of shoeboxes and hangers and

drawers of belts and scarves and other feminine fripperies, he found himself frozen.
Cammie surrounded him. The bright colors
she liked to wear. The fuzzy sweaters that
outlined her modest breasts. The silky wisp
of a nightgown he had bought her in Paris
during a romantic trip he'd combined with
business. She had been so patient with him.
So understanding.

He took a handful of the silk lingerie and
held it to his nose, inhaling deeply, remembering. He was hard, hard as stone. Aching
for something that was not going to happen.
Ever again.

As a man accustomed to running his life
his way...all the time...what he was feeling
now left him gutted. Morose.

With a second curse, he thrust the soft garment away and pulled Cammie's list from
his pocket. The suitcase came down from a
shelf over his head. He stuffed it with pants
and tops and a couple of cardigans. The shoes
she'd requested went in another small bag.

Back in her bedroom, he rummaged in her
dresser drawers, locating bras and panties.

Hell. His hands shook. The rock in his stomach made it hard to breathe.

Doggedly, he continued on to the bathroom to retrieve Cammie's travel kit. He opened it to make sure everything was there. Toothbrush and toothpaste were not bothersome. But the birth control pills gave him pause. Was Cammie seeing someone? A red haze obscured his vision.

He had assumed she was grieving for him. Regretting their breakup. Why would she need birth control if she was home alone every night?

The questioned tormented him for the next half hour as he attacked his chores on autopilot. He found her computer on the kitchen table. Shut it down. Packed it up in a stylish leather tote. Eventually, he was satisfied that he had accumulated everything on Cammie's list. He retrieved her mail, set the thermostat.

As he drove back to his house, his brain spun in a million directions. Cammie was under his roof for a short time. Four or five days…maybe a week at most. What did he want from her? Did he have a subconscious agenda when he'd offered to be the baby's foster parent?

Maybe he did. Maybe he was hoping Cammie would find out how hard it was to take care of a kid. Maybe he could convince her to give up on the pregnancy thing. Cammie was young. She had plenty of time. And in the here and now, she could go to Australia with him. They could see the sights in Sydney, wallow in the sunshine. Make love...

By the time he made it back home, he had convinced himself the plan was rock solid. It took him two trips to get everything inside. The house was dark.

He carried the suitcase and the toiletry case down the hall, leaving everything else in the foyer. The guest room door was closed, but a light shone from underneath.

"Cammie?" He knocked lightly.

She opened the door almost instantly. The baby nestled on Cammie's shoulder sound asleep. Cammie looked beautiful but tired. "Did you find everything okay?" she asked, whispering.

"Sure. How are things here?"

She met his gaze with a fillip of challenge. "Fine."

"I'm glad." The lie threatened to stick in his throat. He didn't want Cammie to think mothering was easy. He wanted Cammie to give the baby back to Officer Lopez and play with *him*... Drake.

He set her suitcase and toiletry bag beside the door. "Your computer and other stuff are in the foyer. Is there anything else you need right now? It's the middle of the workday in Sydney. I have several calls to make."

Cammie's gaze was unreadable. "Pumpkin and I are great. Thanks again for doing your part."

His feet seemed reluctant to move. "The fridge is full. Help yourself if you get hungry. Mrs. Hampton shopped yesterday."

"Drake..."

"Yes?"

"I'm sorry we're intruding. And I'm pretty sure you wish you had never said anything. But even so, I'm glad Pumpkin didn't have to go to some strange family."

Drake grinned. "*Technically*, you're a strange

family, Cam. You don't have a single connection to this kid. Not at all."

"Except that I found him on my car."

"And that means nothing."

"Why are you being so mean?"

It was a fair question. He hunched his shoulders. "Maybe because I'm trying hard not to seduce you."

She blinked, her cheeks flushing. "You can't seduce me. I'm a grown woman. I can take care of myself."

"And you, my sweet, are apparently not savvy enough to know statements like that are a red flag to someone who has shared your bed. Someone who knows the sounds you make when you come. A guy who remembers every curve of your body."

The flush faded. Now Cammie was pale, her gaze tragic. "Don't do this...please. I spent months getting over you...over us. I won't go down that road again."

"We were a perfect match in almost every way. You know it as well as I do."

"Maybe. But fundamental issues are the ones that tear marriages apart."

"Then don't worry about marriage. Lots

of couples enjoy relationships that have expiration dates. You're young. What's your hurry?"

"It sounds like you were *always* planning to dump me at some point. Is that true?"

Seconds ticked by as the room fell silent. Truthfully? In some deep corner of his heart, he had thought Cammie might be the one. He'd been in no hurry to be serious. He thought they had all the time in the world.

But how could he ever contemplate going back to square one? And with his own baby, it wouldn't be only seven years. Fatherhood would be a two-decade commitment. Two damn decades.

"I wasn't always planning to dump you, Cam. But I also wasn't planning for the future. You and I were great. I didn't want to overthink things."

"It's really okay," she said. "I always believe it's a blessing when couples discover their incompatibilities *before* the wedding. You and I were lucky in that way."

"We weren't incompatible," he snapped. "Not at all." They liked the same books and movies. They were both night owls. Each of them hated cilantro and liked medium-rare steaks. They rooted for the same baseball team, and they loved to travel.

Cammie shook her head slowly. "You need a woman who will be footloose and fancy-free with you. Someone who understands your desire to be unencumbered. She's out there somewhere, but it's not me."

"Thanks for making that perfectly clear," he said sarcastically. "But there's another choice, you know. Recreational sex? Two people who know how to push each other's buttons? Pleasure, Cammie. Sheer pleasure."

The flush returned. For a moment he thought he was making headway.

But she took a step backward. A literal step, as if to distance herself from temptation. "You're only here in Royal for a short time, and Pumpkin will only need your official status briefly. For you and me to do anything foolish would be just that. We had our time, Drake, and it was wonderful. But it's over."

Three

When Drake spun on his heel and departed the room abruptly, Cammie sank into the nearest chair, her knees rubbery. Having Drake so close was like a biohazard. He affected her in dangerous ways.

He wasn't even trying to mask his intentions or his desires. The man wanted the two of them to tumble back in bed together. Because it was fun.

And he was right, damn him. It *would* be fun. Unless she admitted that *fun* was a misnomer. Fun was a word for things that were lighthearted and entertaining.

Drake was more than fun. When she was

in bed with him, the world was bigger and brighter. The fireworks were real. The sex was like riding a perfect wave. Summiting the most challenging mountain. Diving into an endless pool and coming up to bask in sunlight on the surface. He made her feel strong and happy.

Gently, she stroked the baby's hair. Her heart turned over in her chest, and her womb clenched with yearning. Ever since she was a little girl, she had wanted a baby of her own. College—and a career in communications—had been rewarding. Being asked by her father to head up the new foundation was even better.

But couldn't she have it all? Was that too much to ask?

The early part of the night passed without incident. Pumpkin seemed to be the perfect baby. He ate and slept, and in between, he favored Cammie with happy burbles.

Around 1:00 a.m., things changed.

Clichés were clichés for a reason. Cammie had often heard someone say their infant *had his days and nights turned around*. The expression never meant much to her until now.

She dozed for a few minutes after the midnight bottle. But Pumpkin was restless. Eventually, he started to whimper.

She knew he wasn't hungry, so she scooped him up and changed his diaper. She even burped him once more for good measure. But the placid infant morphed into a red-faced, squirmy lump.

Nothing she did appeased him…except for walking the floor. As soon as Cammie put him on her shoulder and paced, Pumpkin was happy. He cooed and smashed his face into her collarbone. She was thankful he was happy, but exhaustion threatened to drag her under. Back and forth. Back and forth.

"It's late," she whispered. "Time for all little boys to be asleep."

Half a dozen times she tried to put him down in his bed. She had a system. Ease him onto his back. Hand on tummy. Gradually lift hand and try to back away.

It might have been comical if she wasn't sleep deprived.

No matter how slowly she removed her hand and straightened, the little boy woke up again and again.

"Please, sweet thing," she begged. "Please go to sleep."

She knew there were appointments on her calendar tomorrow, though at this hour, she couldn't remember what they were. Even if it took a few days for the authorities to locate the child's mother, Cammie had the flexibility in her work to shift things around.

But how long could she maintain a hit-or-miss schedule? Her father's charitable foundation was new. Things were just gearing up. With the gala approaching, Cammie would be busy, really busy.

Maybe Drake was right, though she couldn't bear to hear him say *I told you so*. Maybe Cammie's impulsive decision was neither practical nor possible. Most pregnant women had nine months to figure out a plan for work and babysitters and all the rest.

Cammie had jumped into caregiving without a thought for how it would impact other aspects of her life.

At the moment, she couldn't even summon the energy to be stressed about it. Her brain was numb. Her spine ached. All she wanted to do was sleep.

Sometime around two thirty, Pumpkin got really mad. Scary mad. Cammie grabbed another bottle, but he wasn't interested. He wailed.

How did new parents learn to do this stuff? Cammie had tears in her eyes, too. Maybe Pumpkin's mother had abandoned him because she simply couldn't handle it.

Cammie heard a quiet knock, and then the bedroom door opened. Drake was framed there, bare feet, bare chest, tousled hair.

He had probably been *completely* bare a few moments before. She knew he slept nude. The gray knit sweatpants riding dangerously low on his hips were no more than a concession to modesty. Cammie's modesty. It wouldn't have bothered Drake to enter the guest room stark naked.

He ran both hands through his hair and yawned. "What's wrong with him?"

Her chin wobbled. "Nothing that I can tell. He just won't sleep. I've tried everything." Her voice cracked on the last word.

Drake's sleepy expression softened into rueful sympathy. "I'm sorry. You look fried,

Cam. Let me take a turn with him. I'm no expert, but I can walk the halls."

Guilt warred with her survival instinct. Drake had explicitly said the baby was her idea, her project. He'd only furnished the credentials and the house.

On the other hand, if she didn't get some sleep, she wouldn't be able to take care of little Pumpkin tomorrow. "Are you sure?" she asked. Her eyes stung with emotion, and she didn't know why.

"Give him to me," Drake said. "Get in bed and turn out the light." He held out his arms.

Cammie handed over her charge with relief, feeling like the biggest fraud on the planet. For a woman who claimed to want children, she hadn't lasted a single night.

Drake cradled the infant in his arms, managing to look both capable and ridiculously sexy at the same time.

Cammie gnawed her bottom lip. "Come and get me if he won't settle down."

"I will." Drake disappeared with the baby into the hall and shut the door.

For about ten seconds, Cammie nearly

changed her mind. Then she climbed beneath the covers on Drake's sumptuous guest bed and passed out.

Drake settled the kid on his shoulder and walked from room to room in his dark, empty house. He'd slept enough that he was wide-awake. Most of the time he didn't need much sleep, anyway, and now jet lag was adding to the mix. Cammie, on the other hand, liked to get a full eight hours. Which made her latest project flawed from the beginning.

He wouldn't tease her about it. A few minutes ago, when he walked into the bedroom and saw her, his heart had clenched with sympathy. She looked beaten. Defeated.

As much as he wanted her to give up the pregnancy idea, he didn't want to see her get hurt. He patted the boy's back absently. "Take it easy on her, kid. She's in your corner."

The baby was awake, sucking his fist. He appeared to be interested in the tour, though whether or not he could actually see much was anybody's guess. Drake didn't turn on any lights. He was hoping the kid might nod off.

This was the first time Drake had taken a

quiet breath since flying back to Royal. He'd been worried about Ainsley, and then he'd run into Cammie.

Now, in the middle of the night, he pondered his options. He had only booked a week-long airfare, a day of which had been consumed in flight. He had assumed that his stepsister would be on the mend by then. In six more days, business in Australia would be piling up. Meetings, appointments, consultations. Decisions.

He had good people in place, but everyone always wanted the boss.

If Pumpkin's mother or father or both hadn't been located in the next few days, would Drake be able to fly off to Sydney, knowing that Cammie was sleeping under his roof?

More to the point, would his foster parent status be in jeopardy if he left?

With no one around to see him, he sat down in an armchair and propped the baby on his chest, careful to support his neck. "Tell me, kid. Why do women always want babies? You're an awful lot of work."

Pumpkin wriggled around but didn't answer.

Drake continued the one-sided conversation. "Am I a bad person? Fatherhood isn't for everyone, you know."

No response. Drake touched the silky-fine hair—what there was of it. "I want her in my bed. Now. This week. What do you think about that?"

Pumpkin drooled so much Drake had a wet spot on his sternum.

Drake stretched out his legs and flexed his toes, feeling the pull on the back of his calf muscles. Ordinarily, if he woke up at this hour, he might go for a run. Instead, here he sat with a small weight against his middle.

"If I'm honest with her, maybe she'll come around. Of course, you're not helping. All she thinks about is you. I've been sidelined by another man. I guess you're proud of yourself."

Pumpkin yawned comically. He was so small—how did his little mouth open so wide?

Drake let his body go still, hoping the kid would get the idea. The clock on the mantel ticked away the minutes. Eventually, the boy slept.

Rising from the chair was a challenge, but Drake did it. All he had to do was pretend he was carrying a small explosive. One wrong move…

Fortunately, the baby stayed asleep. Drake eased open the guest room door and carefully laid the little boy on his back in the crib.

Drake held his breath. Maybe his luck would last.

When he glanced at the bed, he knew what he wanted. Cammie was beautiful. Her fiery hair was spread across the pillow. He actually trembled, his breath hitching in his chest. The urge to join her was almost overpowering.

Though he had been the one to end the relationship, it had caused him great pain. He approached the bed, his bare feet making no noise at all on the thick carpet. The fabric of her top was so thin he could see the outline of her nipples through the bra.

He couldn't fondle a sleeping woman. But maybe if she woke up…

"Cammie…" He whispered her name, willing her to open her eyes.

She never stirred. Reluctantly, he knew he had to leave. The monitor on the bedside table would wake her if the baby cried out. Even without the monitor, the two beds were close enough that Cammie would hear the boy if he roused.

Drake stood for far too long staring at what he couldn't have. Cammie needed a certain kind of man in her life. Somebody who would stick around Royal. The kind of guy who mowed grass on the weekends or played a pickup game of football down in the park on Sunday.

Even as Drake tried to conjure up such an image, he frowned. Cammie's father was extremely wealthy. That might make Cammie a target for fortune hunters. Men like that would tell a woman whatever she wanted to hear.

He told himself it didn't matter. It was none of his business.

Cammie had chosen a path that didn't include him.

Cammie woke up in a panic, certain that something was wrong. Faint light sneaked in around the drapes, but she was disoriented. This wasn't her bedroom. Slowly, her racing heartbeat subsided. The sound that had awakened her was a baby's small cry.

Tossing back the covers, she jumped to her feet and grabbed a bottle. Had Pumpkin snoozed this whole time since Drake took him and she conked out? It must be so, because when she picked up the baby, sat in the chair and offered him the formula, he gobbled it down as if he hadn't eaten in days.

She cradled his head. "Good boy. You slept like a champ, didn't you?" How long had he been awake with Drake?

Thinking about the way Drake had looked in the middle of the night rattled her. If she hadn't been so exhausted, she might have tackled him to the rug and insisted he make love to her. His bare torso and flat abdomen were even more tanned and toned than she remembered. Australia must agree with him.

It ate away at her to think he might choose to live in Australia permanently. She didn't want to imagine the town of Royal without Drake Rhodes. As long as Drake was in Texas, there was the slightest chance that she might eventually get through to him. Surely, he wasn't as entrenched in his bachelorhood as he claimed.

Even as she thought it, she knew she had to

face the truth. Drake didn't want babies. He probably didn't even want a wife. She would be naive to think she could change him.

Despite all that, she wanted another chance. It was a truth she hadn't fully realized until she saw him striding across the hospital parking lot. How pathetic was that? *He* broke up with her. And she was still holding out hope they might have a future.

When Pumpkin was done eating, Cammie laid the drowsy baby in his bed so she could take the fastest shower on record. When she opened her suitcase, it was a mess. Drake hadn't even attempted to fold anything. With a sigh of exasperation, she pulled out a pair of navy dress pants and a matching yellow-and-navy sleeveless top.

Even if she was not at the office—even if she was babysitting—she sure as heck wasn't going to lounge around Drake's house in sweatpants and a T-shirt. She wanted to remind him of what he was missing.

Her big plan got off to a slow start. When she and Pumpkin made it to the kitchen, Drake was nowhere to be found. A note on the fridge said he had gone to the hospital to visit Ainsley. She hoped Drake's stepsister was improving. He would have told Cammie if Ainsley was still in trouble.

The level of her disappointment at finding Drake not home was way out of line. She had to focus on what was important—Pumpkin. It was up to her to keep the baby healthy and happy until he was reunited with his family.

She juggled him in one arm while she brewed a pot of coffee and made herself toast.

When the doorbell rang, she might have ignored the sound, but it could be someone official, a person with information about the baby. Cammie walked quickly to the front of the house and opened the door. Haley Lopez stood there with an older woman at her side. The beautiful officer smiled. "Sorry to show up unannounced, but this is Ms. Conner from social services. She's required to make a visit and see how you and Mr. Rhodes are accommodating Pumpkin."

"Of course." Cammie stepped back. "Please come in. Mr. Rhodes is at the hospital checking on his sister. But I'm happy to show you the setup."

Ms. Conner smiled. "I'm well aware that

you only became involved with the child yesterday. We don't expect miracles."

Cammie laughed ruefully. "You don't know Mr. Rhodes. He tends to exceed expectations."

When Cammie ushered the two women into the guest room, there was a moment of silence. Ms. Conner looked around the room wide-eyed. "I'm impressed," she said. "But I'm concerned that you might have gone overboard. This child's family will likely be found in a matter of days."

Cammie flushed. "I do understand that. I do. But Mr. Rhodes was determined to make a safe and happy environment for Pumpkin."

Officer Lopez chuckled. "I'd say he succeeded."

Ms. Conner pulled out an old-fashioned spiral-bound notepad. She flipped it open and took a pen from her pocket. "Do you have any concerns, Ms. Wentworth?"

"Concerns?"

"New parents often have a number of questions. Caring for such a tiny infant can be overwhelming." She jotted down something, tore the paper loose and handed it to Cammie. "This is a telephone hotline staffed by volunteers. If you find yourself in any kind of alarming situation, or you're at your wit's end, call that number. No need to feel alone."

Cammie throat tightened. Knowing there were people out there ready to help new moms and dads was touching. "Thank you," she said.

Haley Lopez held out her arms. "May I cuddle him for a moment?"

"Of course." Cammie watched as the other woman cooed and bounced little Pumpkin.

"Is there any progress in finding his mother… or both his parents?" Cammie asked.

Haley grimaced. "We thought we had a lead. A Jane Doe came to the hospital the same night as the multicar pileup on the interstate. But there was so much commotion, we can't trace which ambulance brought her in. Or maybe she came in on her own. She's still unconscious. But of course, it doesn't make sense that the baby wasn't with her. Unless she abandoned him and *then* was in the wreck. The trouble is, the times don't line up. We know when you found the baby, and we know when the wreck occurred. It doesn't seem possible that anyone involved is connected to Pumpkin."

"Are there other leads?"

"Not at the moment. There's an additional complication. The Jane Doe at the hospital does not appear to have given birth recently. So the doctors are baffled. But don't worry. We have several investigators on the case. They're taking this very seriously."

"I'm not worried for me," Cammie said. "It's Pumpkin I'm concerned about. He's so little. I don't want him to forget his mom or his dad."

Ms. Conner tucked the pad back in her purse. "Children are resilient. And you're here to give him security and comfort in the short term. It's hard for a person to simply disappear in this age of technology. Someone will be found."

After the women said their goodbyes and the house was quiet again, Cammie walked the hall with Pumpkin until he fell asleep. When he was settled, she powered up her computer and answered emails for half an hour. Then she called her father.

For some reason, she didn't tell him about

the baby. If things dragged on, she would have to eventually. But for now, she didn't want to hear all the reasons why fostering an abandoned baby was impractical and a hindrance to her career.

Her father might have become more generous after Danae's death, but he was the same difficult man, essentially. He wouldn't like his daughter getting involved in a messy situation like this one. And he would definitely raise an eyebrow to hear that Cammie was staying in Drake's house.

Drake didn't make it home for lunch. Cammie found a container of homemade chicken salad provided by the housekeeper. Eating with one hand was becoming easier. Pumpkin was content to nestle in her arm.

She talked to him a lot. Was that weird? Maybe all moms did that.

Sweet little Pumpkin was fast becoming important to her. As much as she understood that he wasn't hers to keep, it was impossible not to let the tiny infant steal a piece of her heart.

She and the baby were playing on the king-size bed in the guest room when Drake finally returned home. It was midafternoon. No hospital visit lasted that long. It was a good bet that Drake was avoiding her.

Even so, he didn't try to pretend she and the baby weren't there.

She heard footsteps in the hall, and then he appeared in the doorway. "Hey, there," he said, his expression guarded. "How are things here?"

Something about that searing blue gaze always made her weak. "Good." She tickled the baby's foot, not wanting Drake to see how he affected her. "A woman from social services came by for an unannounced home visit to make sure we had everything set up for Pumpkin. Officer Lopez was with her. We passed with flying colors, thanks to your shopping spree."

He ran a hand across the back of his neck as if her comment embarrassed him. "Money makes things easier. I was glad to do it."

"What about you?" Cammie asked. "What have you been up to today?"

She was hoping her question might cause him to squirm, but he didn't seem flustered. "I spent more time with Ainsley than I planned.

She's fighting an infection. Spiking a fever. The docs are trying to pin it down."

Now Cammie herself felt guilty. "I'm so sorry. I didn't know she was worse."

"I don't think she's in serious danger, but they always worry about stuff like this. Of course, she's eager to come home, but they won't release her until she's out of the woods. If the appendix hadn't ruptured, it might even have been outpatient surgery."

"I'll write her a note. You can take it when you go the next time."

"She'd like that. When you and I were dating, Ainsley told me it was the first time I had shown good taste in women."

Cammie laughed. "I always did like your stepsister."

Drake still hovered in the doorway. Maybe he thought getting too close to the baby would give him cooties. "My friend is one of the chefs at the Bellamy," he said. "I've ordered a big dinner for you and me. Someone will deliver it around seven. Do you think Pumpkin might sleep while we eat?"

"I have no idea," Cammie said. "I think he's too young to be on a schedule yet. But if he won't sleep, I can hold him." Drake grumpy expression was comical, though Cammie hid her smile.

"I had in mind something a little more romantic," he said.

Cammie's throat dried. She had to be strong. After a moment, she weighed her words and spoke. "I would enjoy having dinner with you, Drake. But a chaperone is probably a good idea. I'm not willing to do *anything* romantic with you. It's out of the question. The only reason I'm here is because you're a legal foster parent and Pumpkin needs your credentials."

Now Drake's face was wiped clean, no expression at all. He seemed calm, relaxed. "The price for my sponsoring him was to have you under my roof. And you agreed. You can't be entirely surprised if I press my advantage."

Her heart fluttered in her chest. His dogged insistence that there was something left of their relationship both alarmed and exhilarated her. "I didn't think you were the kind of man to force yourself on a woman, Drake Rhodes. Shame on you."

Her reprimand didn't make a dent in his sexy confidence. Nor did the lock of dark hair that refused to stay in place. It fell over his forehead, giving him a rakish air.

His wicked smile sucked all the air out of the room. "Force won't be necessary," he drawled. "When you end up back in my bed, it will be because neither of us can resist. I'm a patient man, Cam. But I can't wait to hear you cry out my name when I make you come."

Four

Drake wanted to laugh at the look of shock on Cammie's face, but he didn't dare. He was playing a dangerous and uncomfortable game. The more he teased and taunted *her*, he more his hunger grew. He'd been awake for hours the night before, stingingly aware that the woman he wanted slept just down the hall.

His impulse to bring the abandoned baby to his house had been just that, impulsive. But he soon realized that his libido had been shouting directions from the back seat. Having the home field advantage when it came to Cammie was too valuable to ignore.

He straightened and gave her his best innocent smile. "I'm going to take a shower. All those hospital germs, you know. After that, I'd be happy to watch the monitor while the kid is asleep. I assume you have work piling up."

Cammie nodded slowly. "Yes. But I thought you didn't want to have anything to do with him."

Drake shook his head slowly, feeling wry amusement. "I think I can manage to glance at a tiny screen. You can trust me, Cammie."

"Okay." She chewed her bottom lip, a sure sign she was agitated.

"Is there a problem?"

"I'm sorry if I was rude about dinner."

"You weren't rude. You merely put me in my place. *No funny business.* I got the message, Cam."

Pumpkin was safely in the middle of the huge bed. Cammie stood and crossed the room until she was so close to Drake their breath mingled. "You're toying with me," she accused. The flush on her cheeks and the fire in her emerald eyes told him she was worked up about something.

He touched her nose with a fingertip. "I've missed you."

Cammie was not wearing shoes. She had to tilt her head back to look up at him. Her eyes were a softer green now. Or maybe he was reading her expression wrong. Maybe he was seeing things that weren't there.

Her shoulders rose and fell in a deep sigh. "I've missed you, too." Her tone was reluctant, as if the admission had been pulled from her unwillingly. She cupped his cheek with her hand.

His heartbeat stilled. "Touching me is probably not smart," he said hoarsely. It was the God's honest truth.

Her thumb traced his chin. Her gaze was troubled. "That was always the problem, wasn't it? Neither of us was smart when we got lost in each other. I still care about you, Drake. Maybe I always will. But I can only be your friend. Yes, I'll have dinner with you tonight. But I won't sleep with you."

He held her hand to his face, feeling the delicate bones in her wrist. *This* was one reason he had gone to Australia. He'd needed to put half the globe between himself and temptation. When he found himself unable to speak, Cammie went on.

"Did you offer to be Pumpkin's foster parent so I would come to your house and sleep with you?" she asked.

He swallowed hard. "No."

"Did you do it because you felt guilty about our breakup and wanted to make me happy?"

He nodded slowly. "Yes."

In a startling move, she went up on her tiptoes and kissed him lightly on the lips. It was a quick kiss, barely any contact at all. But the small caress seared its way to his soul. He caught a whiff of her familiar scent. She broke the contact and stepped back. "I appreciate what you've done. But that's all the more reason for us not to muddy the waters. You're a good man, Drake. You were honest with me. And now we both know where we stand. Why on earth would we want to mess that up by having sex?"

"Because it would be fun?"

"Oh, Drake." She must have thought he was joking, because she laughed softly, her expression affectionate.

"That isn't reason enough?" It sure as hell was for him.

"You have your business and Ainsley and

probably half a dozen willing women around the world. Pumpkin and I will only be here for a few days. There's no need to complicate things. I don't want to be at odds with you. I'll be ready to eat by seven," she said.

Drake wanted to argue, though Cammie wasn't wrong. They were finally at a good place. Maybe he would back off for now, but she couldn't ignore the heat between them. It was a living, breathing creature.

If he was patient, the situation might take care of itself.

Cammie rocked Pumpkin, holding him close. He had taken a bottle greedily. Now he was almost asleep in her arms.

She ought to receive an award for her acting skills. Lying to Drake had been an exercise in desperation. She did want to sleep with him. Desperately. But it wasn't that simple. He was literally a man on the move. If she gave him emotional control of her happiness, he would break her all over again.

Drake wanted a temporary sexual relationship.

Cammie needed far more from a man.

When Pumpkin's head lolled on her arm, she rose to her feet and laid him gently in his crib. "Where is your mother?" she whispered. "Surely she didn't abandon someone as sweet as you." The facts said differently.

In the luxurious bathroom, Cammie freshened up. Her beautiful silky top had a spot of spit-up on it. She wanted to change clothes… wear something more suited to an intimate dinner. But if she was serious about not having sex with Drake, she shouldn't give him mixed messages.

Earlier, he had been as good as his word. For two hours, Drake had kept the monitor with him as the de facto parent on call. Cammie had thus been free to sit at the kitchen table and work without interruption. She had accomplished so much she no longer felt so stressed about her job and her schedule.

Making a face at herself in the mirror, she took a washcloth and removed the dried milk. Then she brushed her hair and twisted it up on top if her head. Why was she so nervous? It was only a meal with a man who used to be important in her life.

Her bravado lasted all the way down the

hall but fell apart when she found her host in the dining room. Unlike Cammie, he *had* changed clothes. Dark pants and a pale gray dress shirt with the sleeves rolled to his elbows made him look sexy and relaxed. The fact that his feet were bare emphasized his masculine appeal.

When Cammie entered the room, he looked up and smiled. "Just in time."

She eyed the largesse on the beautiful table. "How many people did you invite?" she asked, teasing him.

"Just the two of us."

Beef medallions in burgundy sauce. Sautéed squash. Asparagus tips. Thin cheddar biscuits. A bowl of beautifully cut strawberries with fresh cream. Cammie sat down and put her napkin in her lap. "Clearly, I ought to patronize the Bellamy more often than once a year. Honestly, during the height of the pandemic I ordered carryout so much, I forgot how nice it is to eat in a great restaurant."

Drake joined her at the table. "This is carryout, too," he said ruefully. "But I didn't think you would enjoy taking a baby to the Bellamy."

"You are so right. I don't imagine my fellow diners would care for it, either."

"Unless Pumpkin slept through dinner."

"There are no guarantees," she said, filling her plate. "This is much nicer."

They shared the meal in harmony for at least twenty minutes. But with each passing moment, Cammie became more convinced she had to ask the question that had haunted her for months. "Drake," she said, taking a sip of her wine for courage.

He looked up, his expression relaxed. "Yes?"

She hated to ruin the mood. "I've been wanting to ask you something. A question I should have asked two years ago."

Now his gaze was guarded. "Then why didn't you?"

"I don't know." She shrugged. "It didn't seem important at the time." Maybe it still wasn't, but with Drake pushing the issue of their sexual relationship, she had to understand why he had ended things before.

He sat back in his chair and crossed his arms over his chest. "Spit it out, Cam. I've never known you to be a coward."

She swallowed hard, her mouth and throat

dry despite the wine. "Tell me why you don't want to have babies. I'm not judging you," she said quickly. "And I'm not trying to change your mind. But I don't get it."

Drake didn't look angry, and he didn't look upset. If anything, his expression was resigned. "It's no big secret," he muttered, rotating his head on his neck. He clearly regretted his demand for honesty.

"It is to me," she said quietly. "I'd like to know."

He shrugged. "Ainsley," he said simply. "She cured me."

"I don't know what you mean."

"Think it through, Cammie. Ainsley was fifteen when she was orphaned. No family at all besides me. She was literally on the verge of becoming another teenaged statistic in the system. But she was my stepsister. I couldn't let that happen. So I went through the process, got certified and became a foster parent."

"Okay…"

"A sane person would be grateful, don't you think?"

"And Ainsley wasn't?"

"My God, no. She was furious. Lashing out at anyone in reach."

"And you were the closest target."

"Indeed. I took my college exams early, moved out of the apartment I shared with a friend and came home to Royal. Bought this house. Let Ainsley fix up her room any way she wanted. I didn't take her in to win any points, but it wouldn't have killed her to say thank you now and again."

"She was hurting."

"I *know* that. And I knew it then. But even knowing didn't make it easier. Fifteen-year-old girls can be hard to handle in the best of situations. Ainsley was a brat. And maybe she had reason to be, but our relationship was hell."

"I'm sorry, Drake. You never talked much about your past with her."

"I was still almost a kid myself when I did the foster parent thing. At twenty-two, I was ready to take on the world. I wanted to travel and have lots of sex and find out who I could be. But I was stuck in Royal."

"Where, by the way, you shot your way to the top of the business scene in no time. You found success early, Drake. And you clearly did a great job raising Ainsley."

"I got lucky in both instances."

"You have an incredible brain and a big heart, even if you don't want to admit it. Surely Ainsley quit fighting you at some point. When you and I started dating, she was super sweet to me."

"You saw the good side of our relationship. Things had mellowed by then. Even so, I can't ever forget the hard years. Until she graduated from high school and went off to college, I thought I might lose my mind. Being responsible for another human being is a huge burden. I did it once. I don't want to do it again."

The tone of his voice and the harsh certainty in his words told her the subject was closed. He went back to eating his meal. By the look on his face, he tasted nothing.

Cammie made herself finish the food on her plate, but she felt nauseated. This was not a man who was going to change his mind. He'd had a traumatic experience when he was a young adult, and he'd been marked by it.

She summoned a smile, trying to salvage

the evening, though she was heartsick. "New subject. Tell me what you're working on in Australia. I have only the vaguest idea."

His body language relaxed visibly. "I'm diversifying my financial consulting business with an entirely different approach in Australia. Actually, Ainsley gets some of the credit for the idea. You probably know she graduated from college in the spring. All she wanted to talk about was how to help her classmates who were floundering. They didn't want to live with their parents, but they couldn't find the kinds of jobs that would enable them to be independent."

"Maybe they wanted too much. Don't most young adults struggle to find their footing? My dad supported me, but he insisted I work a couple of minimum-wage jobs, just so I would understand how hard life can be, even with a college degree."

"You were lucky."

"Yes. So what's this big new approach?"

His grin was boyish and full of enthusiasm. It was also sexy and unfair. Why did he have to be so damn charming? His creativity and determination were two of the qualities that had attracted her in the beginning. He was a fascinating man.

"I'm teaching college kids how to invest," he said.

She stared at him. "You're joking, right?"

"Not at all. They can start with as little as five bucks a week, and if they have the discipline to keep at it, they can potentially retire young and have a sizable nest egg. I'm working on an app to make it even easier."

"And why Australia?"

"I met a guy at a conference. He and I hit it off. When we were brainstorming, we came up with the app idea. He's from Australia, and he says the twenty to twenty-nine age group is over fourteen percent of the population. So we have a big pool of potential customers. Plus, who wouldn't want to spend time in Australia?"

Her heart sank. "Are you thinking about moving there permanently?"

"Maybe. I doubt it. But anything is possible. You'd love it, Cam." He gave her a winsome smile. "I was hoping to convince you to go back with me for a few weeks."

She cocked her head, frowning. "Hoping when?"

"Yesterday. Last night. I've missed you."

"And what about my job and Ainsley and Pumpkin?"

"Problems can be solved. Plans can be changed."

"Maybe in your world. Not mine. You're talking crazy."

He reached across the distance separating them and took her wrist, pressing his fingertip to the spot where her pulse beat rapidly. His usually sky-blue eyes darkened to midnight, the irises almost eclipsed. "I never could think worth a damn when you were around. Tell me you don't remember what it was like between us. I dare you."

That *was* the problem. She did remember. Vividly. "I know what you're saying, Drake. I do. But there's more to life than physical compatibility." Strangely, she couldn't summon the energy to pull away from him. He made her weak. His allure shattered her common sense. She trembled violently.

When Drake rose to his feet and tugged her arm, she stood, too. He rubbed his thumb over her cheekbone, the intimate gesture destroying all the reasons she wanted to keep her distance. "I want to kiss you, Cam." The words were ragged, unsteady.

"Oh…"

"Is that a yes or a no?" The words were teasing, but his expression was grim, his features etched in granite. "Be honest, Cammie. Tell me what you want."

There it was. The chasm. Reason and good choices on one side. A night with Drake Rhodes on the other. But that was crazy. She could kiss him and stop after that. One kiss didn't have to lead to hours of debauchery.

Drake grew frustrated with her silence. She could see it in his eyes. But her lips wouldn't move. Her voice wouldn't work.

Now he took her by the shoulders, his grip firm but careful. "Tell me. What. Do. You. Want?"

It wasn't easy. But it was inescapable. From the moment she saw him in the hospital parking lot, she had wanted this. "Kiss me," she muttered.

The air sizzled in a moment of shock. His fingers tightened on her skin, hard enough to bruise, perhaps. He went entirely still, like a predator waiting for the perfect moment. "Are you sure?" he asked hoarsely. "You have to be sure."

"Oh, for heaven's sake." She put her hands on his cheeks and pulled his head down, dragging his mouth to hers. "I want you. There. I said it. Are you happy now?"

He made a sound low in his throat, a sound that had the hair on her arms standing up in an atavistic recognition of danger. His lips ground against hers, smashing against her teeth, stealing her breath. Joy slammed into her chest, incredulous joy.

Inhaling sharply, she breathed in the essence of him, shivering at how well they fit together. This was bad, really bad.

Drake's body was hard and warm against hers. His hands roved across her back, tugging her closer. Between them, his erection was impossible to miss.

She had imagined a kiss that was filled with poignant regret for things past. A kiss of goodbye. A kiss that acknowledged all the ways a relationship between two such dissimilar people was doomed.

Apparently, Drake had a different agenda. He kissed her wildly, in turns tender and demanding. It was as if the two years they had been apart vanished into the mist.

Leaning into him, she found home. But no, that wasn't true. Drake wasn't her home. He didn't want to be responsible for her. He didn't want to make babies with her.

When he tangled his hand in her hair and loosened it, she knew she was skating into dangerous territory. Something about a man taking down a woman's hair was as intimate as removing her clothes.

Pins scattered on the carpet. Cammie was hot suddenly, too hot, despite her sleeveless top and Drake's top-of-the-line HVAC system.

An insistent voice inside her head told her it would soon be too late. She and Drake were wildly aroused, hungry. And this was no initial encounter. They were each well aware of what came next. Endless, drugged pleasure. Again and again.

He pulled back, his broad chest heaving, his breath ragged. "I want you in my bed, Cammie."

No matter how destructive the impulse was, she couldn't say no to him. "Yes," she whispered. "Yes."

The flare of heat in his gaze was matched by his triumphant smile. She couldn't find it in her heart to care.

He pressed his lips to her forehead. "I should take you here on the table," he said, "so you won't change your mind."

Cammie nipped his bottom lip with her teeth. "I won't change my mind." She wanted to be naked with him, wallowing in the way he made love to her. All virile intensity and demanding testosterone. It was what she had always wanted.

A dark flush rode high on his cheekbones. He stripped off his shirt. "Plan B, Cam. My bed is too far."

With a sleight of hand that startled her and made her gasp, he unzipped her expensive pants and had them down and off in a nano-second. Next went her top. Now she stood there in front of him wearing heels, panties and a bra.

He went still, his gaze riveted on her barely covered breasts. "You're exquisite, Cam."

He touched her nipple, fingering it lightly through a barrier of lace.

Cammie was startled to realize that his hand trembled. Did she really have that power over him? Or was it something they generated together? A drunken, wildly passionate response that had nothing to do with alcohol and everything to do with the desperate way they wanted each other.

"You're right," she whispered. "The bed can wait." Carefully, she unzipped him and stroked his length.

His breath hissed through clenched teeth. "Cam…"

"Yes, Drake?" She smiled, drowsy from the large meal and eager for dessert.

He stepped out of his slacks and kicked them way. His navy boxers barely contained his excitement. When he removed them, Cammie felt like a scandalized Victorian maiden. He was big, and he wanted her badly.

She reached behind her back and unfastened her bra. When she dropped it on the carpet, she saw Drake's Adam's apple shift as he swallowed.

His grin was feral. "Bend over the table, darlin'."

Cammie laughed. "Kinky…" She turned to follow his outrageous command, humoring him, because it pleased her. As she spread her arms, she knocked the baby monitor onto the floor.

Everything in her body froze. Nausea and mortification rolled over her in equal measure. "Oh, no," she cried out.

Drake touched her arm. Not at all sexual. "Easy, Cammie love. Nothing is wrong. He hasn't made a sound."

Cammie was in shock. In her headlong rush to reunite with her lover, she had completely forgotten about little Pumpkin. What kind of person did that? Cammie was supposed to be the woman who wanted a baby more than anything. And yet, when Drake crooked a finger, she lost all reason and metaphorically abandoned the precious little infant in her care.

Wildly, she scrambled to pick up her clothes and the monitor. Tears, hot and dreadful, drenched her cheeks. She felt sick and wounded. With everything in her arms clutched to her naked chest, she faced him. The man who wanted her body but not her future.

"You did this," she said, her heart broken into a hundred nasty pieces. "You wanted to prove to me that I don't have what it takes to be a mother."

He took a step in her direction, his expression tight. "No, babe. Calm down. Nothing happened."

Cammie was humiliated, embarrassed beyond belief. Drake had seen her naked before. That didn't bother her. But the fact that he'd witnessed her failure as a parent—maybe even knew it was happening and didn't care—destroyed her.

"Move out of my way," she said, her voice hoarse.

Drake held out his arms. "Let me hold you, Cam. You're upset."

She narrowed her eyes. "Damn right I'm upset. You used sex to prove a point."

"That's not even rational, honey. We both got caught up in the moment. It was natural and wonderful. Parents have sex, you know."

His joke fell flat. She sucked in a breath and shoved past him. "I'm not a parent, and neither are you. Pumpkin and I will go to a hotel tomorrow."

Drake caught her by the shoulder and whirled her around. His eyes flashed. "You can't do that. *I'm* the one with the foster care credentials, remember?"

"I hate you," Cammie cried.

He crossed his arms over his chest, flaunting his nakedness. "You can try telling yourself that, Cam, but we both know it's not true."

Five

Cammie opened the door to the guest room with exquisite care and sneaked in, like a teenager coming home late and trying not to get caught. She dropped her clothes on a chair and tiptoed across the room to stand by the crib, her pulse finally settling to something approaching normal.

"I'm so sorry, Pumpkin," she whispered. "I didn't really forget about you. Well, maybe just for a minute. But you have to understand. Drake Rhodes is a force of nature. He makes me do crazy things."

The baby slept peacefully, his tiny hands fisted beside his head.

It was getting late. Pumpkin would be wanting a bottle soon. Did she have enough time to take a shower? Surely so.

She wanted to erase every last vestige of Drake's touch from her body. She was *glad* they hadn't actually had sex. Truly, she was.

When the baby didn't stir, she went into the bathroom and shut the door. A hot shower restored some of her equilibrium. She didn't wash her hair. It took forever to dry, and it was a good bet she didn't have that long.

Would Pumpkin do a repeat of last night? Or would he let his temporary mama get some sleep? While Drake had kept watch this afternoon and Cammie worked on her computer, she had taken a few minutes and done some reading about the various stages of newborns. Things could change quickly. It was possible for a child at six weeks to begin sleeping in five-hour stretches.

Cammie could handle that. It was the non-stop crying that was hard. And of course, she didn't know exactly how old the baby was.

There was no point worrying about what might or might not happen.

By the time she was ready for bed, Pumpkin had woken up. Cammie sang to him while he took his bottle. After burps and a dry diaper, she played with him on the big mattress. Thankfully, he lasted only thirty minutes before his eyes closed.

Once he was settled in the crib, Cammie made a beeline for her own bed and climbed under the covers. She was sleepy, but even as she drifted off, Drake was there with her. Kissing her, teasing, ready to make love all night.

Why wouldn't he leave her alone?

Why couldn't *she* forget about what they had once shared?

Please God, let Pumpkin's family be found soon before Cammie did something she would regret.

The next morning followed a familiar pattern. Cammie fed the baby, dressed both of them and discovered that Drake was gone. His bedroom door stood open. The bed didn't look as if it had been slept in.

What happened last night after Cammie fled? Where had he gone? It was silly to worry about a grown man, but her unease continued.

When she went to the kitchen for her coffee, she was embarrassed to see the housekeeper bringing dishes of congealed food from the dining room.

Cammie's face flamed. "I'm so sorry," she stuttered. "I should have dealt with those last night."

The pleasant older woman shook her head. "Nonsense. This is my job. You're supposed to be taking care of that little cutie. Drake told me the whole story." She dried her hands on a towel. "May I hold him while you have a bite of breakfast?"

Cammie smiled. "Of course."

Drake's housekeeper, Mrs. Hampton, cradled the baby in the crook of her arm. "He's precious." She touched a tiny finger. "I had four of my own, but it's hard to remember they were ever so young."

"He's an easygoing baby. I hope they find his mother soon."

Mrs. Hampton shot Cammie a glance. "It's good of you and Mr. Rhodes to look after him."

"Well, he *was* found on my car," Cammie said. "I know there must be a dozen or more good foster parents in Royal, but I couldn't bear to let him go."

"You like babies?"

It was a simple question, not at all judgmental. But Cammie felt defensive. "I do. I want to have at least two of my own someday."

"Any prospective daddies in the picture?"

Mrs. Hampton had been around a long time. She had met Cammie when Drake brought her home as his girlfriend several years ago. So was this a leading question? Was the woman prying? Or was she simply asking?

Cammie leaned against the counter, feigning relaxation, though her mood was unsettled. She took a sip of her coffee to wash down the delicious bite of Danish that stuck in her throat. "No one special at the moment. But I hope he's out there for me. If not, I'll give single parenting a try."

"It's hard," the other woman said bluntly. "My husband was in the army. Deployed all over the world. I was a good military spouse, though at times I couldn't help but resent his freedom. At least he got leave occasionally. I had two little ones in diapers and no life to speak of...nothing but hard, hard work."

"I'm not afraid to work," Cammie said. But suddenly she flashed back to the night before last when Drake had rescued her. She had been at her wit's end with a baby who wouldn't sleep. A single parent carried all the responsibility.

Pushing aside her worrisome thoughts, she held out her hands. "I need to give him a bath," she said. "I have my sink all set up. Wish me luck."

"Do you need a hand?"

"No, but thanks. I think I've got this."

In the guest bathroom, Cammie gave the baby a stern look. "Don't make things too hard for me, kiddo. I'm already scared of dropping you. Give me a break, and we'll both make it through this just fine."

Pumpkin blinked sleepily and drooled bubbles as if to say he knew Cammie was a fraud. *Aren't you the same lady who forgot I existed last night, because you were fooling around with your ex-boyfriend?*

"We're not going to discuss that," Cammie

said. "And besides, I learned my lesson. *You* are the only man in my life from now on."

The bath was not without hazards. Still, Cammie was determined. It probably took twenty minutes longer than it should have, but eventually she had the squirmy baby on the bed—clean, diapered and almost into a soft, warm onesie.

The door to the hall was open. Mrs. Hampton knocked anyway. Cammie fastened two more snaps, careful not to pinch skin. "What's up?" she asked over her shoulder.

"There's someone here to see you, Ms. Wentworth."

"Call me Cammie, please." Cammie picked up the baby and put him on her shoulder. "It's almost time for his bottle."

"It's a young woman about your age— Sierra Morgan? Says she gave you her business card a few days ago?"

Cammie's heart sank. She sighed. "Yes. I've met her."

"I put her in the living room and offered her a glass of tea."

"Thank you, Mrs. Hampton."

Cammie picked up the sweet-smelling infant. "Here we go, sweetheart. Let's hear what she has to say."

Sierra Morgan was as beautiful as Cammie remembered. Petite, long blond hair, green eyes. Though her appearance was soft and vulnerable, Cammie had a hunch the woman was far tougher that she appeared.

That hunch was reinforced when Cammie sat down, and Sierra immediately peppered her with questions. "Hi, Ms. Wentworth. I'm here to do a story about the abandoned baby for the *Royal Gazette*. Have you heard from the child's mother or father? How's the little one doing?"

Cammie held up a hand. "Whoa. Stop right there. First of all, it's Cammie, not Ms. Wentworth. And second of all, what's the deal? You told me you work for *America* magazine."

"I do. And I agree. Last names are pretentious. Please call me Sierra. I'm still preparing the big piece about the upcoming gala and the anniversary of the TCC finally admitting women. Anyway," she said, "this baby thing caught my attention. I spoke to someone at the *Gazette*, and they're willing to run the story with my byline."

"But why you, Sierra? You're an outsider. What is it about this situation that makes you want to get involved?"

Sierra had an odd look on her face for a moment, but it vanished, replaced by determination. "Why not me? Besides, *you* certainly got involved. Far more than I have. I guess most people are suckers when it comes to protecting innocent babies."

"Fair enough." Cammie was a bit taken aback by Sierra's enthusiasm and push to get the story told. Cammie didn't want to give up Pumpkin yet. Though she knew a newspaper article might be the infant's best chance of being identified, she was uneasy about sensationalizing Pumpkin's plight. What if the publicity brought out some of the crazies who liked to benefit from other people's misfortunes?

Sierra picked up on Cammie's ambivalence. "Don't worry. I'm not going to say a word about you and Mr. Rhodes. No one needs to know where Baby John Doe is living at the moment."

"We call him Pumpkin," Cammie said. "He needed a name."

"I like it." Sierra smiled. "Very seasonal." She paused. "But honestly, I'm going to concentrate on when and where he was found and reach out to the community for possible clues. We'll include the appropriate phone numbers for the police department. The story will generate buzz, and that will be in Pumpkin's best interests."

"Maybe." Cammie noticed something odd. Most women couldn't resist playing with a newborn. Sierra hadn't made any move to indicate she wanted a baby cuddle. "Would you like to hold him?" Cammie asked.

This time, Cammie knew she didn't imagine the flicker of *something* in the other woman's gaze…a certain bleakness. Maybe regret.

"Not really," Sierra said with a strained smile. "He's happy. I don't want to spook him. I'd rather concentrate on why I'm here."

Sierra didn't give Cammie time to analyze the reporter's demeanor. She pulled out a notebook and threw out more questions. After the seventh or eighth *I don't know*, Cammie sighed, exasperated. "I swear…you know as much as I do. You were there…remember? I doubt you can make a Pulitzer Prize–winning piece out of a handful of details."

This time, Sierra's smile was the real deal. "Don't worry. I can make a story out of a pencil and a verb. It's in my blood." She stood and slung the strap of her bag over her shoulder. "You still have my card, right?"

Cammie stood as well, bouncing Pumpkin in her arms. "I do."

"Well, then, just shoot me a text if any new information comes to light. We need to reunite this little one with his mama."

The reporter's words were absolutely true. No reason for Cammie to feel threatened. But she clutched the baby a little tighter. "Hopefully, soon," she said, acknowledging if only to herself that she was a fraud. Already, the thought of handing over sweet Pumpkin to someone else made her stomach hurt. The baby was happy with Cammie. Was she a bad person if she hoped the hunt took a little longer?

The afternoon passed quickly. While the baby napped, Cammie ate a packet of peanuts and worked on her computer. The structure of the Danae Foundation was coming along. Although she was not directly involved in planning the gala, her father's money would be an integral part of the night's festivities.

About four o'clock, Drake returned. Pumpkin was asleep. Cammie was working in the den. Drake walked into the room and dropped onto the love seat beside the sofa where she sat. "I'm sorry," he said quietly.

"For what?" She wasn't quite able to look at him. Last night's debacle was too fresh. The memory made her shudder with embarrassment.

He sighed. "I stepped over a line. I'm sorry I tried to pressure you into doing something you didn't want to do."

It would have been so easy to let that statement stand. To let him think everything was his fault.

She shook her head slowly. "That's not what happened. I could have walked out of the room at any time. I didn't. Because I wanted you, Drake. I still do."

His eyes flashed with shock. "But?"

"But I know that passion burns out. Compatibility is the thing that keeps relationships alive."

"Maybe we can agree to disagree."

"Maybe."

After an awkward moment of silence, he motioned to her computer. "Is it rough this week having to be away from work? Are they being accommodating?"

Cammie realized that Drake didn't know her circumstances had changed. "I don't work for the oil company anymore."

His eyebrows went up. "Oh?"

The last time the two of them spoke—before Drake went to Australia—Cammie had still held her position as VP of public relations with one of Royal's big oil companies. It had been an interesting job, and she liked to think she was good at it, but she knew she had made the right decision.

Drake was waiting for an explanation.

She grimaced, wondering if he would judge her. "My father created a charitable foundation and named it after Danae. He made me the executive director."

"Is that what you wanted?" He watched her

carefully, as if trying to peer inside her soul. She didn't want him psychoanalyzing her.

"I didn't ask for it, if that's what you mean. But the job has turned out to be very exciting and challenging. I'll tell you a secret, if you swear you won't say anything."

He mimed locking his lips. "You can trust me."

It was true. She could. With everything but her heart. Shaking off the maudlin thought, she tucked her legs beneath her and closed her laptop. "The Danae Foundation is planning a big reveal at the TCC gala in tandem with the club and the hospital. That's why I was there when we ran into each other. A select group of first responders from fire and emergency services as well as hospital workers are going to be inducted as honorary members of the Cattleman's Club."

"Wow. That's pretty forward thinking for such a rigid social pecking order."

"But about time, don't you think?"

"No question." He leaned forward, hands on his knees, clearly interested. "Those people put their lives on the line after the tornado in 2013, and more recently with COVID." He paused. "So where does your dad come in? And the new foundation?"

Cammie smiled, her heart filled with pride. "My father is paying the college expenses for all the children of the people being honored."

Drake blinked. "Holy hell. I've met your father. This doesn't sound like him."

"I know, right? Danae really changed him, both when she was alive and after her death. I'm thrilled, frankly. My father has far too much money anyway. This is the least he can do. I'm hoping his gift will go a long way toward repairing the Wentworth reputation. We could use a little bit of good press."

"No offense, but your dad has alienated more than his share of Royal's citizens."

"Maybe everyone will take his generosity seriously and give him a chance to mend fences and make a new start."

"Let's hope so." Drake seemed dubious.

Cammie wasn't insulted. She knew that people in towns like Royal had long memories and sometimes held on to grudges. Her father had made mistakes. Big ones. But she liked to think Danae had put him on a better path. Maybe, even now, Danae was looking after him from beyond the grave.

Because Cammie was the tiniest bit freaked out about how her father's largesse would be received at the gala, she changed the subject. "I assume you've been to the hospital. How's Ainsley doing today?"

Drake leaned back in his chair and propped his feet on the ottoman. When he laced his hands over his flat abdomen, Cammie shivered inwardly. He was a beautiful man. Intensely masculine. Almost arrogantly confident. Sexy and impossible to resist.

Did she want to have sex with him? He would be leaving soon. Maybe she should go for it. One last time. For closure.

How was that for rationalization?

Her thoughts made her antsy. Was she about to do something stupid?

The object of her obsession looked half-asleep, but he answered her question. "She's fine. Much better, in fact. The doctor says they can probably release her day after tomorrow if all her labs are good."

Cammie's heart sank. Once Ainsley came home, there would be little privacy in this house. He wouldn't be able to spend all his free time trying to seduce a woman he broke up with two years ago.

"I'm glad to hear she's on the mend," Cammie said. "What else did you do today? You've been gone a long time."

For the first time, Drake looked uneasy. "Well…" He stopped, rubbed his chin and sat up. "I had to give someone a tour of the ranch."

Her gut clenched. "Why?"

He shrugged. "A potential buyer."

Cammie was shocked to her toes. This house Ainsley lived in was only one of Drake's homes. He also owned a huge, fabulous spread outside town. She shook her head slowly. "You love that ranch."

"I do." His jaw was outthrust. Clearly, he didn't want to talk about this, but Cammie was alarmed.

"Then why would you even consider selling?"

"You know that my manager has been running the place for several years now. I've lived temporarily in New York and now Australia.

It seems impractical for me to hold on to the ranch. Things change. Life moves on."

Cammie went cold inside. Her fingers gripped the arm of the sofa. "Does this mean you might move to Australia for good?"

He scowled. "What does it matter to you, Cam? You've been pretty clear about the status of our relationship."

"*You* broke up with *me*. I still care about you, Drake."

"Meaning what?" His tone was challenging. Almost belligerent.

Cammie had thought finding a baby on her car was a watershed moment in her life. But that paled in comparison to this new information. Drake might leave *permanently*. How could she bear it? She took a deep breath and searched for words. "Feelings can't be turned off like water faucets," she muttered.

His expression lightened. "You have feelings? Who knew?"

"Don't mock me," she snapped.

"I wasn't, I swear." His gaze softened. "But you're so easy to tease."

"I don't want you to live in Australia," she whispered.

Now it was impossible to read his expression. He stood and rested one arm on the mantel. "We've barely spoken in the past two years. Why does it matter where I am?"

His gaze was laser focused. He watched her intently.

Cammie didn't like it. Why should *he* be allowed to know what she was thinking? But on the other hand, her time was running out. Either Drake would get on a plane, or Pumpkin's family would show up, or both. Cammie would be alone again.

She had a brother who wouldn't come home to Royal, a mother who preferred her life in the big city and an emotionally unavailable father who was grieving. Cammie had an active social life, sure. But it hadn't escaped her notice that one by one, her girlfriends were getting married and *settling down*.

She hated that phrase. It sounded too much like *settling*.

"It matters," she said slowly, "because I liked knowing I might run into you on the street. I liked knowing we saw the same sunrises and sunsets. You're part of Royal, Drake. An important part."

"That makes me sound like a lamppost or a restaurant."

"You know what I mean," she muttered. She had waded so far into this conversation that she couldn't find her way back out.

Six

Drake found himself in quicksand. He had missed Cammie, far more than he was willing to admit. Two years ago, he'd told himself that cutting her loose was the kind thing to do. But his noble gesture, if indeed it was that, had cost him deeply.

"I don't know what you want from me, Cam." It was the truth. He was frustrated in more ways than one, his emotions on edge. He didn't like this feeling.

She sat like a child with her legs crisscrossed now. But she was a woman. A vibrant, sexually appealing woman who still had the power to turn him inside out.

When he didn't say anything else, she picked at a loose thread on the sofa cushion and scowled at him. "Tell me the truth, Drake. If we hadn't bumped into each other in the hospital parking lot, were you planning to find me and say hello?"

The quicksand deepened. He sensed the question was a deal breaker. But he wouldn't lie to her. "I don't honestly know. I was focused on Ainsley and getting home as fast as I could. I had work things to tie up, too. It probably crossed my mind, but you weren't at the top of my list as I was leaving Australia."

Almost immediately, he regretted his candor, but his answer didn't appear to have upset her. She nodded slowly. "Fair enough."

"What does that mean?"

"It means I'm thinking."

"About what?"

She shrugged. "About whether or not I'm going to sleep with you."

Her matter-of-fact statement was a blow to the chest. He wasn't accustomed to parsing his sexual entanglements so dispassionately. He was more of a live-in-the-moment kind of guy when it came to sex. Come to think of it, weren't most men?

He swallowed against a dry throat. "I'd be happy to weigh in…"

Cammie wrinkled her nose. "No doubt." She cocked her head and stared at him. "Have you changed your mind about not wanting a family?"

The question caught him off guard. "Not even a little." He blurted it out without thinking and was immediately sure that he had destroyed any chance of coaxing her into his bed. Was he stupid?

Cammie stood and crossed the distance between them in two graceful strides. When she was close enough for him to inhale her scent, she stopped. "Okay."

He was befuddled. "Okay, what?"

She placed one hand, palm flat, on his chest. "Yes, I'll sleep with you. We have tonight and tomorrow before Ainsley comes home the next day. Let's make the best of it. Since you're probably moving to the other side of the world, this will be our last chance." She rubbed his lower lip with her thumb. "Kiss me, Drake. Please."

The next few minutes were a blur. He slid his hands beneath her hair, feeling clumsy and desperate. If she changed her mind, he wasn't sure he could bear it. Being in this house with her, so close and yet not together, had tormented him.

When his lips found hers, the air around them sparked. Twenty-four months faded away, Suddenly, it was Cam and Drake again. Perfect. Hot. Erotically charged.

How could a kiss be so deeply arousing when both of them were fully clothed?

He was seconds from stripping her bare when the baby monitor emitted an unmistakable sound. "Damn it..." Drake jerked backward, nearly hitting the mantel with his shoulder. He wanted to howl in frustration. He was hard and ready.

It made him feel the slightest bit better to realize that Cammie was equally flustered. She smoothed her hair where his hands had ruffled it. Her cheeks were flushed. A red scrape on her throat marked the spot where he had nibbled on her. "I'm sorry," she said. "Obviously we'll have to wait until tonight. But anticipation is half the fun, right?"

Her expression said she didn't really believe that.

He ground his teeth. "Go get him. Feed him. Whatever he needs. I'm going for a run. I'll pick up pizza on the way back."

When he stalked out of the room, Cammie didn't try to stop him. She didn't say a word.

Drake changed clothes quickly and exited the house by a back hallway. He didn't want to see Cammie. He felt volcanic. It wouldn't take much to make him say something unforgivable.

He wasn't jealous of a helpless infant. He wasn't.

The route he chose was a familiar one. Occasionally he saw someone he knew, but he cut through side streets to avoid talking to anybody.

He ran, and he ran, and he ran, until his chest hurt and his eyes burned. Knowing he was about to do something selfish made him ashamed. What Cammie offered, he would take, knowing full well he couldn't give her what she needed in return.

Did it matter at all that he had been honest?

Were the scales of justice balanced because he hadn't lied?

No matter how many miles he covered, the answers to those questions eluded him.

When he had been gone almost an hour, he forced himself to turn around. Cammie would be hungry. He had promised dinner. Surely, he shouldn't—wouldn't—add to his list of failures.

Leaning against the side of a building, panting, he pulled out his cell and ordered a pizza. Then he summoned a rideshare and hoped the driver wouldn't take one look and pass him by. Drake was covered in sweat and still had a stop to make on the way home.

Fortunately, the young man who showed up six minutes later wasn't inclined to be critical. He was, however, a talker. Drake wanted desperately to lean back and close his eyes, but it wasn't to be. The kid rattled on for the whole trip. Even when Drake hopped out to get the pizza, the monologue started up again as soon as he returned to the neon-green Kia.

Drake paid on the app and added a thirty-dollar tip. It wasn't the driver's fault that his passenger was in a lousy mood.

Back at home, he showered, well aware that the pizza was getting cold. Why didn't he have it delivered? Apparently, his brain was shot.

He dried off, threw on jeans and a soft Henley shirt, and scooped up the box. At least it was still marginally warm on the bottom.

Cammie was in the kitchen with the baby. She had put together a salad and set the dining room table. Her expression was guarded when Drake appeared. "I didn't know what you wanted to drink," she said.

Wine would have been his first choice, but he needed a clear head. "A Coke is fine." When she passed him on the way to the fridge, he caught her shoulder, pulled her close and nuzzled her neck. "I'm sorry I left. I was feeling…" He trailed off. How could he describe his disappointment? It would make him vulnerable to her.

Drake needed to be in control of the situation, didn't he?

Cammie managed to soothe the baby and stroke Drake's hair as if she had been juggling two males her whole life. "I was frustrated, too," she said simply. "But little Pumpkin didn't know he was ruining our fun."

Drake straightened. Had it been something as simple as *fun*? He didn't think so.

Cammie stepped away, and the moment passed.

Over ham-with-mushroom pizza and soft drinks, they talked of random, easy things. The weather. The local football team's winning season. The way Ainsley had waited too long to admit she was hurting. How scared Drake had been when the doctor called to let him know what was going on.

"You know you're a fraud, right?" Cammie said, tempering the words with a grin.

"What do you mean?"

"You talk about how terrible it was to become Ainsley's guardian, how your relationship was toxic. But the moment something happens to her, you drop everything and fly halfway around the world to be by her side. You love her, Drake."

He drained his glass, avoiding Cammie's perceptive gaze.

When he looked up, she shook her head slowly, her expression filled with affection.

He didn't want that from her. He wanted mindless, perfect sex.

Cammie must have sensed his discomfort, because she changed the subject. "If you'll hold the baby, I'll clean up the table. I'm not leaving it for Mrs. Hampton again. I don't want her to think we're pigs."

Drake chuckled, taking Pumpkin and nuzzling the baby's head with his lips. "She's my *housekeeper*, Cam. I don't think it's out of line to ask her to clean up the dining room and kitchen."

"Maybe not, but I want to do it anyway."

Suddenly, a memory popped into his head. He and Cammie had been at her place, ready to make love. But Cam had insisted on tidying the remains of their meal. At the time, he hadn't given a flip. The chores could have waited.

His lover had insisted.

Cammie was always the more responsible of the two of them when it came to mundane jobs around the house. She actually seemed to like it.

He'd never given that quirk in her personality much thought until now. Maybe her chaotic childhood had given her a need for order. And maybe he should be more aware and not protest when his wants and needs had to wait.

He rubbed the little boy's back. "You're the man of the hour, kid. I got bumped to second place."

Drake knew the baby didn't understand a word he was saying. Besides, it was a joke.

It was a pleasant evening, so he took the baby outside for a breath of air. Pumpkin seemed interested in the sights and sounds. Birds sang in the maple tree near the sidewalk. A light breeze stirred the branches of the huge live oak.

It occurred to Drake that he might as well deed this place over to Ainsley. That way she would have roots and a home of her own. There was plenty of room in the house for Drake to stay when he came home for a visit.

And what about the ranch? It literally hurt to think about selling it. But if he wasn't going to live here in Royal, why would he keep it? For an investment? Maybe. Still, the way he felt about the ranch had nothing to do with money.

He heard the front door open and shut.

Cammie came down the steps to join them. "What does he think of the big ole world?" she asked, smiling.

She seemed calmer suddenly. Happier.

Her mood relaxed some of the tension in Drake's neck. "I think he likes it."

To anyone driving by, they must look like a family. Drake winced inwardly. He handed Cammie the baby. "I'm pretty sure he needs a diaper. I could do it, but you're faster."

She rolled her eyes. "That's the worst excuse I ever heard."

"What can I say? It's not my thing."

Cammie tucked the infant against her shoulder and murmured something to him. The words were so low, Drake didn't quite catch them. She looked sideways at him. "Does *anybody* like poop? It's just one of those things you have to deal with in life. Like the dentist and doing your taxes."

He chuckled. "How about I do your taxes and you handle Pumpkin?"

"Fine," she huffed, pretending to be annoyed. But the light in her eyes told him she wasn't truly miffed. "Are you coming inside?"

"In a minute," he said.

When they were gone, he shoved his hands in his pockets and walked the perimeter of the property. Here in town, the lots were average size. No houses crammed together, but certainly not the acreage he had out on the ranch.

He had grown up in Royal. Gone to school here until college. Returned to finish raising Ainsley and start a business. Ainsley was an adult now. His financial interests continued to diversify and grow. With every passing year, he had more and more reasons to travel the world and fewer to come back to this town.

Could he leave it all? Australia was amazing. He had loved his time there and was eager to get back.

But not without Cam.

The trouble was, she was firmly rooted here. This town, this land, these people. She loved them all.

And she wanted a baby. It was that simple and that complicated.

He shoved the conundrum out of his mind and went inside, counting the hours until the baby fell sleep again. Then Cammie would be in Drake's bed.

He found them in the den. Cammie sat on the rug with Pumpkin on a soft blanket beside her. Drake paused in the doorway, watching them unnoticed.

Cam tickled the baby's tummy. "Are you too little to laugh for me? I know you are. Where's your mama, little boy? What is she doing? Is she scared? Hurt? Why did she leave you on my car?"

The baby made little burbling sounds, but he didn't answer a single question.

Drake joined them on the floor. He leaned back against the sofa and tugged Cammie into the vee of his legs. "The witness is stone-walling you," he said.

Came leaned her head against his chest and sighed. "Yep. I love taking care of him, but I know he needs his family."

"Did you hear anything from the police today?"

"Same old, same old. Haley Lopez called. They're investigating. Told me to be patient. I just don't understand how it could happen. And why it's taking so long to find the baby's family. It's the twenty-first century. Nobody can go off the grid easily."

"True. But maybe the mother doesn't want to be found. Maybe she planned this for some time."

"I suppose."

Pumpkin seemed happy for the moment, so Drake bent his head and traced the shell of Cam's ear with the tip of his tongue. She groaned and shivered in his arms.

"I want you, Cammie. Quite desperately, in fact."

She half turned in his embrace, searching his face. Her beautiful moss-green eyes sparkled with passion—passion he wanted to stoke. She touched his cheek. "I want you, too, Drake. I've missed you. And don't worry. I know what this is that we're doing. I'm glad we cleared the air."

Her words created an odd, unpleasant feeling in the pit of his stomach. Instead of taking issue with what she had said, he found her mouth and covered it with his. She tasted like pizza and possibilities.

Their tongues dueled lightly. He held her chin in his hand, keeping her faced tipped up to his. The position was awkward. He wanted to feel her soft curves against his chest.

With his free hand, he found her breast. She was wearing another thin top, this time with a flirty short skirt. How had he not noticed that before?

Once he began exploring, there was more good news. Her legs were bare. The only thing underneath the skirt was a pair of undies that were silky against his fingers.

He touched her intimately, all the while deepening the kiss.

His lover whimpered. Even so, it was Cammie who called a halt. She put a hand against his chest and pushed. "It's too soon, Drake. We can wait."

"Not soon enough," he muttered, disgruntled.

Trying to ignore the ache in his rigid erection, he released her and stood. "How much longer till he's asleep?"

"Thirty minutes, maybe more. And I need a shower."

He took her hand and pulled her to her feet. "Will you come to my room? When you're ready? I'll be waiting for you."

* * *

Cammie second-guessed herself a thousand times in the next hour. She was both excited and terrified. The memory of how her relationship with Drake had ended was still fresh in her mind. She had cried a million tears. Her self-confidence had shattered. Her heart barely survived.

And now she was going to wallow in his bed, well aware that they weren't a couple. Even knowing how this would end, she couldn't help herself. Being with Drake was what she wanted, no matter how self-destructive.

Pumpkin was in a cooperative mood. He took his bottle easily, burped a couple of times, cooed and played for fifteen minutes, and then zonked out. She laid him in the crib and stared down at him. Was it possible to love someone who wasn't yours?

Sadly, she was walking down that road with two males—one, this baby who would eventually be reunited with his blood kin, and two, Drake, who would soon walk away. Or fly, to be more accurate. Why was she allowing either one of them to have a piece of her heart? If she was smart, she would guard her emotions.

Unfortunately, she had never learned that trick. Her parents and her brother knew how to be aloof, unreachable. Cammie had thrown her love all over the place. Childhood friends, schoolmates, teachers. She had a soft heart, and she expected the best of people. It might not be the safest way to live a life, but she didn't know any other.

It wasn't her fault that she'd been hurt and disappointed over the years.

She wouldn't change who she was, even if she could.

Once she was convinced that Pumpkin was soundly asleep, she took a quick shower. Afterward, she debated what to wear. At home in her closet, she had several sexy, beautiful sets of lingerie. Silky nightgowns. Flirty satin robes. When she asked Drake to pack for her, she certainly hadn't directed him toward those.

Now she was sorry.

Since she couldn't do glamorous tonight, she opted for comfort. She chose an old, soft football jersey in navy and red. One of her high school boyfriends had gone on a college visit and brought it back to her. The teenage beau was long out of the picture, but Cammie had a particular fondness for the jersey.

It hit her midthigh. She brushed her hair and left it down.

Her heart pounded so rapidly, she thought she might be sick. Why hadn't she asked Drake to come to her?

With one last look at the baby, she picked up the monitor and stepped into the hall. The house was silent. Beneath her bare feet, the hardwood floor was cold.

Drake's bedroom was two doors down. First a guest powder room, then the master suite. She knew it well. When she opened the door and entered, the luxurious space was empty. For a moment, she was rattled. Then she saw the ribbon of light beneath the bathroom door.

A few seconds later, before she'd had time to catch her breath, Drake exited, wearing nothing but a damp towel wrapped around his hips.

He smiled when he saw Cammie. "Good timing."

Her throat closed up, making it impossible to speak. To disguise the fact that she was mute, she turned and set the baby monitor on the corner of a beautiful chest of drawers. At the moment, she was standing as far as possible from that massive, hedonistic bed. A taupe duvet, lightly embroidered in gold, covered the mattress.

Drake had turned back the covers on one side, revealing the inviting cream cotton sheets. Large, fluffy pillows rested against the headboard.

One corner of his mouth ticked up in a tight grin. "You look terrified, Cam. Am I that scary?"

She shifted from one foot to the other. "No."

It was an unconvincing lie at best. She held her breath when he crossed the room and took her hands in his. Her fingers were icy cold. His were firm and warm.

"We're still us," he said simply. "Nothing has to be weird."

She searched his face, looking for reassurance. She knew Drake felt *something* for her. Something more than sexual desire. They shared a history. He was fond of her.

It was a terrible time to realize that she was still in love with him. The sudden jolt of awareness made her heart sink. How could she have casual sex with this gorgeous man and not give away her secrets?

Nothing had changed in two years. She had tried to convince herself she was over him…that her wounds had healed. Deep inside, though, on some subconscious level, she had always known. Drake Rhodes was her one and only. She adored him despite the fact he had broken off their relationship. She loved him, even knowing he didn't want her love.

Why else would she have begun to think about in vitro fertilization? Or adoption? If she couldn't have Drake as her husband and the father of her theoretical baby, she didn't want any man in her life.

A child would give her the chance to start a family. A nontraditional family, sure. But was she hurting anyone? No…

Drake must have misunderstood her long silence. He pulled her close, wrapping her in his embrace. The way he held her was both comforting and wildly arousing. How could it be both?

He kissed her forehead. "Talk to me, Cam."

His body was so much bigger than hers. The difference in their heights was pronounced, especially since she was barefooted.

"I'm ready," she said, wanting him desperately.

"It's not a calculus final, darlin'. We're not doing this unless you're all in."

She realized in an instant that his big frame was tense. Beneath her cheek, she could feel his thunderous heartbeat. Could he possibly be as uncertain as she was?

She went up on her tiptoes and pressed her lips to his. "I want to have sex with you, Drake, truly I do."

Seven

Drake didn't believe her, not entirely. But he chose to take her words at face value, even as they gave him pause. The old Cammie would have said *make love*. It was a tiny but important difference.

He knew she didn't love him now. That was part of the price he paid for breaking off his relationship with her. His motives had been altruistic, but he hadn't counted on how much it would hurt to have his sweet Cam look at him with disdain all those months afterward.

She *had* loved him back then, but he had thrown it all away.

These past months in Australia, he'd had

plenty of distractions to occupy his attention. Getting a new business off the ground chewed up the hours and days. Royal had seemed like another lifetime.

All that changed when he saw Cammie again. He understood how carefully he had sublimated his desires, how intentionally he had blocked the memories. Perhaps he'd been in blatant denial. Or maybe he hadn't wanted to admit he'd fucked up.

Now, finally, he was so close to getting what he wanted.

Shaking off the past, he stripped off the jersey Cammie wore and scooped her into his arms to carry her to the bed. He knew the exact moment she spotted the pile of condoms on the nightstand. But she didn't say a word.

As he set her gently on the big mattress, Cammie scooted over to make room for him. Drake ditched his towel and joined her. He groaned as he pulled her into his embrace and held her. "You feel so damn good," he said as his body tangled with hers. All arms and legs and beating hearts. She was soft everywhere he was hard.

He kissed her ravenously, ruefully aware that he felt more like a beast than a man. His mood was wild, his control tenuous at best.

When he moved on top of Cam, she wrapped her arms around his neck, smiling up at him, the smile of a siren, a temptress. "You're a hard man to resist."

"If it's any consolation, you came close to turning me into a drooling idiot. You're even more beautiful than before, Cam. Since the first moment I saw you in that hospital parking lot, I've wanted you. Badly."

The intensity of his words seemed to bother her. Her gaze shifted away. "Well, you have me," she said.

"Maybe I'm the one who's scared," he joked. "A two-year break is a lot of pressure. I don't want to disappoint you." *Not like I did before.*

"You know very well that you're good at sex. I'm sure even the women in Australia have figured that out."

Was she fishing? He cleared his throat, not sure how to respond. "I haven't been celibate since we broke up, Cam. But my sex life is not as…*varied* as you seem to think. And certainly nothing serious."

She held up a hand. "Not my business. Kiss me, Drake."

Something about her demeanor worried him. Was she seriously trying to convince herself this was only sex? He cared about her. A lot. Maybe *showing* her was his only option.

Now that he had her in reach, he found the patience to slow down. He kissed her gently, from her cute nose to the sensitive spot on the arches of her feet and everywhere in between. The intimacy was rich, familiar. Completely alluring. He and Cam had always been like this, their bodies in tune, one person's passion feeding the other.

Cammie gasped and writhed beneath his touch. Her soft moans and the way she arched her back made him feel like he could fly.

He buried his face in her taut belly, inhaling her scent, trembling at the prospect of being inside her again after so long, far too long.

Her nails dug into his shoulders when he stroked her with his finger. She was hot and wet, her body ready for his.

When he would have made her come, she pushed him away. "Not until you're inside me, please."

She didn't have to ask twice. With shaky hands, he rolled on protection. Then he moved between her legs and pressed at her entrance. "I want you, Cam." The words were guttural, forced from somewhere deep. Was *wanting* enough?

When she pulled his hair and lifted her hips, he got the message. He surged hard, making both of them catch their breath. The sensation was exquisite. His eyes burned. How had he lived without this?

Carefully, he stroked deep, resting his weight on his elbows, staring down at her, trying to memorize her face. He kept up the lazy pace until she came apart in his arms. His own climax was not long after. He shouted her name and hammered wildly, wanting to mark her as his.

The world came crashing down on him. He was emotionally and physically exhausted. Everything went black.

When he woke up sometime later, Cammie was gone.

* * *

Cammie was pleasantly sore and completely satisfied. See…that wasn't so bad. She could do casual sex. She had just proved it.

When she had heard Pumpkin waking up, she wasn't sure how long she had been asleep. The monitor was set loud enough to rouse her. But Drake never moved.

That was fine. It was actually better this way. She didn't need his help with the baby. After diapering and feeding the boy, she stroked his forehead until the little guy went limp in her arms. By now, she was better at putting him down. Or maybe he was better at sleeping. Either way, this middle-of-the-night feeding went smoothly.

After Pumpkin was settled, Cammie dithered. She didn't quite have the courage to saunter down the hall and climb back into bed with Drake. But she knew he would be pissed if she returned to her own bed.

While she was deciding what to do, Drake appeared in the doorway, yawning.

He kept his voice low. "Everything okay?"

She nodded, feeling off kilter but not unhappy. Being with Drake again had been wonderful. "Yes. He ate and went right back to sleep."

"Splendid." Drake's sexy smile curled her toes. He came to where she stood in the middle of the room and tucked her hair behind her ears, kissing the side of her neck. "Let's not waste a moment."

After they returned to the master suite, the night took on a surreal feeling. She and Drake napped in short snatches, then made love again and again. He was tireless. And hungry. As if she had somehow been depriving him of what he wanted.

When the sun came up, she groaned. Her little charge was once again making his presence known.

Drake lifted up on one elbow. "Go back to sleep, Cam. I can handle a turn."

She shook her head, rattled at the idea of being out of it when the two men in her life were awake. "Oh, no. It's my job. I'll do it."

Her lover leaned over her and kissed her hard. "You'll need your rest for later," he said, the words slurred with fatigue and promise. "Sleep, angel. I'm being completely selfish, I swear."

"Are you sure?" She brushed the hair from his forehead, unable to separate the torrent of emotions she felt.

"Completely." He rolled out of bed and exited the bedroom.

What neither of them had counted on was the fact that Cammie could hear everything happening in the guest suite. When Drake murmured to the baby and soothed the fussy infant during a diaper change, Cammie heard. When he hummed a silly song and settled into the rocker to give the child a bottle, Cammie heard.

Her heart broke into little pieces. How could a man capable of so much care and tenderness be so stubbornly opposed to having a family?

But then again, there was a huge difference between offering temporary foster care and doing the long-haul parenting thing. Despite her pain, she could barely think straight. Sleep claimed her, promising sweet oblivion.

Drake yawned, keeping one eye on the baby, who tried to stuff his fist in his mouth. Pumpkin was growing and changing every day. Drake and the infant were on Cammie's bed, doing nothing in particular.

Cammie needed at least another half hour. Drake did, too. But since Cam had handled the middle-of-the-night feeding, it was definitely his turn.

When even sitting up straight was too much, Drake sprawled on his back and slung one arm over his face. Beside him, the baby was happy. Lucky kid.

The world was a much easier place when all a guy needed was milk and naps.

Before last night, Drake had entertained a hazy, half-formed plan where he and Cammie would screw every time the baby slept. But he now saw the flaw in that plan. Babies demanded attention. Drake and Cammie were in bad shape. Sleep deprivation was going to make this a very long day.

He had drifted off for a moment when a small, feminine hand shook his shoulder. "Wake up," she whispered.

"I've been watching him," he said quickly, feeling his face flame. "I wasn't really asleep, I swear."

Cammie grinned. "He's fine. It's a huge

mattress. We won't be in any danger of rolling over on him."

Drake scrubbed a hand across his face. "We?"

"Scoot him over and let me in."

"Okay." He felt befuddled. He knew adults weren't supposed to let infants sleep in the same bed with them. But that was during the night—right? Surely a quasi-nap wasn't dangerous.

He moved the baby with extreme care. Then Cammie slid in and pulled the covers over herself.

Drake frowned. "How do we know he's not cold?"

"He's not. That sleeper is very thick and warm. And he has socks on *under* the sleeper. He's fine, I swear. Touch his cheek and his hand if you want to be sure."

Though Drake felt a bit foolish for worrying, he did as Cammie suggested. The baby definitely didn't seem cold. Drake slid closer to Cammie and joined her under the covers. "It seems mean not to cover him up."

"I know. But it's a safety thing."

Drake closed his eyes. His body hummed

with arousal, though it simmered at a comfortable level. Right now, he was tired enough to enjoy cuddling Cam.

They drifted in and out, neither of them willing to sleep deeply when the baby was awake. But eventually, Pumpkin slept, too.

Cammie's body was soft and warm. Drake spooned her, lifting the hem of the football jersey she wore to feel her ass. Predictably, his boner grew.

"I have a confession to make," he mumbled, reaching under the jersey to palm her breast.

"Oh?" The single syllable was breathless. Cammie wriggled, nestling her butt into the cradle of his groin more perfectly. Surely, she had to feel his erection.

Drake's forehead broke out in a sweat. "I thought we would probably have sex today every time the kid napped. But I guess that's not practical. We'll have to get some sleep eventually. We sure didn't last night."

Cammie rolled onto her back. Her eyelids drooped. Her cheeks were flushed. "We can sleep when we're dead."

Her naughty grin shocked and elated him. "Hell, yeah."

"But we can't do it right beside him," Cammie said.

She was right. "And we don't want to risk moving him," Drake said.

"And we can't go to *your* room while he's not in the baby bed."

"Well, hell…"

Cam reached under the covers and found his hard-on, stroking him lightly. "Why don't you go grab a condom?" she whispered. "I'll meet you on the floor."

Her suggestion galvanized him. He rolled over her and off the bed. It was a clumsy move, but he was desperate. By the time he returned less than two minutes later, Cammie had found a soft, fuzzy throw and spread it on the floor beside the bed. She was sprawled, buck-ass naked, on her back.

When Drake froze in the doorway, stunned by the erotic display, she held a finger to her lips. "Shh. Don't make a sound."

"Duly noted," he said, dropping to his knees beside her. Though he was as hard as he'd ever been in his life, he paused to appreciate the feast. The thing that pleased him most was Cammie's smile. She looked happy to see him.

Never again would he take that for granted.

He sat back on his heels and stared.

After a span of seconds that felt like an eternity, Cammie blushed everywhere it was possible to blush. "Stop that," she hissed. "Come down here and warm me up."

"Yes, ma'am." They rolled together on the throw, trying to be quiet but failing when Cammie wouldn't stop giggling.

Finally, he put a hand over her mouth. "If you wake the baby," he said, "I'll have to spank you."

Her eyes went wide. She nodded.

Drake didn't move his hand. Instead, he managed protection awkwardly, nudged her thighs apart with his knee and balanced on one elbow. "Not a sound, darlin'."

It was a silly game. She could easily have dislodged the fingers that covered her lips. But Cam played along. Her faux docility ratcheted Drake's chest-heaving hunger.

When he finally managed to get inside her, his heart pounded so loudly in his ears, he felt dizzy. She was completely still, as if moving equated noise. Come to think of it, with Cam, it probably did.

He flexed his hips, gaining another inch. His silent lover made a sound deep in her throat. Barely audible. Rife with need.

He wanted to laugh, but he couldn't. This felt damn serious.

Because he needed to read her expression, he finally uncovered her mouth. Nuzzling the side of her neck, he pumped slowly. "Wrap your legs around my back, Cam. Hold me tight."

She did as he demanded, locking her ankles and making it possible for him to go deeper still. He had blocked this out of his mind. How good it was. How hot and sweet in equal measure.

Cammie wasn't saying anything. But then again, who needed talk when the physical connection was damned near perfection? He kissed her hard. "I can't stop screwing you, darlin'. As soon as we're done, I want you all over again."

She curled one hand behind his neck and pulled him down for another kiss. "I'm not complaining."

The smug, teasing joy in her voice sent him over the edge. Vaguely, he was aware that Cammie found release at almost the same moment. She buried her face in his shoulder, but even so, her muffled cry was audible.

They lay there, panting. Their skin chilled as the sweat dried. At last, he lifted off her, rubbing his face. "Can we get on the bed without waking him?"

"Maybe." She groaned. "I'm getting too old for the floor."

He extended a hand. "I would say I'm sorry, but it would be a lie."

Gingerly, they slipped onto the bed and pulled the covers up again. Cammie rested her cheek against his rib cage, her hand splayed across his abdomen. "That was nice."

Stroking her hair, he tried to summon indignation. "Nice? Come on, Cam. Surely you can come up with a better adjective."

"Don't be greedy." She yawned. "We should grab a few minutes of sleep while we can. I can't guarantee how much longer he'll be out."

Twenty minutes. The answer was twenty minutes. Cammie and Drake had fallen into a deep unconscious state when she heard the baby stir. She tried not to cry.

Her head throbbed, and her eyes were gritty. It was going to be a long day.

Drake woke up seconds after she did. He groaned. "You may be too old for the floor, but I'm definitely too old for all-nighters."

She took a deep breath. "Why don't you shower and get dressed while I feed him? Then you take a turn. And no sleeping in the bathroom."

"Very funny."

When Drake disappeared down the hall, Cammie found her robe and shrugged into it, tying the sash tightly. Her muscles were sore, and her body was tender in surprising places. She wanted to smile at the memories, but Pumpkin was not prepared to wait while his temporary mama mooned over the man who had made her body sing.

Cammie grabbed a bottle and carried the baby to the rocker. When she was settled, she offered the meal to him, smiling when he gobbled rudely. Didn't he know it wasn't polite to slurp in public?

Despite how she and Drake had joked about

the subject, it wasn't practical for the two of them to fool around all day. For one thing, the lack of sleep would make them zombies. More importantly, Cammie found herself wanting to draw back, to protect herself.

Last night and today with Drake had been both exhilarating and deeply painful. To contemplate what her life could be like with the man she loved was a lesson in futility. Drake had been nothing but honest with her.

He was going back to Australia. For an indefinite time. And if he ever decided to come back to Royal for good, Cammie couldn't marry him even if he asked. Which he wouldn't. She had made no secret of her maternal hopes and dreams.

Drake wanted none of it.

Pumpkin had just reached the end of his bottle when Drake returned, looking handsome and fresh and far more chipper than Cammie felt. His hair was damp from his shower. He was wearing soft, faded jeans with a pale-yellow cashmere sweater that emphasized the breadth of his chest.

Instantly, Cammie felt frumpy. Her hair

was a mess. She needed a hot shower to wash away the evidence of her night with Drake.

He took the baby from her without asking. "I'll burp him and walk him. Go do whatever you need to do."

When Cammie stood, Drake pulled her close with one arm. He kissed her right on the lips with the baby watching. The kiss was long. Lazy. Filled with promise.

Both adults were breathing heavily when it was over.

Cammie stepped back. "I won't be long," she promised.

Drake bounced the little boy gently. "The menfolk will entertain ourselves, right, Pumpkin? And we'll throw together some breakfast."

When they walked out of the room, Cammie gathered clean clothes and headed for the bathroom. Hot, steamy water washed away some of her mental fog. She shampooed her hair and shaved her legs.

Afterward, she used the dryer she found under the sink to restore order to her long hair. Soon it was shiny and soft on her shoulders. She sat down at the counter and applied light makeup. Subtle eye shadow, a quick coat of mascara.

She didn't really know why she was taking such pains except that anyone might drop by the house this afternoon. And though Drake had seen her rumpled and with bed hair, she wanted to present herself in a more flattering light.

When she was done, she followed her nose to the kitchen, inhaling the life-giving aroma of expensive coffee. Drake waved a hand. "It's ready. Will you pour me a cup, too?"

He looked entirely natural with a baby on his shoulder.

"Sure."

Somehow, he had managed to butter toast one-handed. He'd chosen to use a cookie sheet in the oven instead of the toaster. A few of the edges were too dark, but Cammie wasn't about to complain. Especially when Drake produced a bowl of strawberries from the fridge to go with their feast.

Her stomach growled loudly.

Drake chuckled. "Somebody burned a lot of calories last night."

He seemed totally relaxed, as if nothing out of the ordinary had happened. But Cam knew better. She had indulged wantonly, despite the risks. Because she couldn't say what she really wanted to say, she chose to keep her face buried in her food.

They ate without speaking after that. Only baby sounds broke the silence in the kitchen.

Cammie could almost see the tension building. Part of it was sexual, no doubt. But there was more. Between them, a host of painful truths danced and mocked.

Soon Pumpkin would be sleepy again.

Suddenly, Cammie couldn't imagine sharing Drake's bed in the cold light of day. Her emotions were raw, her heartbreak too close to the surface. What was she going to say? They had agreed to indulge last night and today. A sort of last hurrah.

The truth was, she was done. The need to get away from Drake was urgent and real.

For once, he didn't pick up on her mood. The man she loved was oblivious to her distraught mental gymnastics. She wasn't allowed to take the baby and leave. Drake wasn't going to move out of his own house.

Cammie was trapped by circumstance and her love for him.

They had almost finished cleaning up the kitchen when Drake's cell phone rang. Cammie took the baby so he could answer.

She watched his face change. And she listened without apology, though the guts of the conversation eluded her.

When he hung up, she cocked her head. "What is it? What's wrong?"

His jolly mood had paled. His expression was hard to read. "That was Ainsley," he said. "The doctor is so pleased with her progress they're releasing her earlier than they thought. Today. After lunch."

"Oh." Cammie's heart sank, even as her common sense told her this was for the best. "That's great news. I know you were worried about her."

He showed his hands in his pockets. "Cam?"

"Yes."

"I thought we had more time to talk and, well, you know."

"It's okay. We had what we needed."

He scowled. "What does that mean?"

"Closure. A chance to end things on a better note."

Eight

Drake strode into Royal Memorial Hospital, trying to ignore the panic-stricken rage swirling in his gut. He desperately needed an outlet for his frustrated anger. In other circumstances, he would have stopped by the gym to go a few punishing rounds with the punching bag.

Closure? What kind of lame-ass word was that? He and Cammie had spent an amazing night together, and now she was talking about *closure*? That was bullshit.

Earlier, after the call from the hospital, Cammie had disappeared with the baby, leaving Drake to wallow in his own dark mood.

To go from sexual satiation to the cold knowledge that she was brushing him off made him feel sick. They had been getting along so well.

What was up with her? He would never understand women, damn it.

In the elevator, he inhaled and exhaled, trying to pull himself together. It wouldn't do for Ainsley to think he was upset or didn't want her to come home.

Before he entered her room, he pasted a smile on his face. Then he opened the door. "Hey, my little chick. How ya feelin'?"

Ainsley was still pale, but her grin was genuine. "Not my old self, but definitely ready to get out of here."

He put a hand under her chin and tipped up her face. "You look better. More *interestingly frail* than at death's door."

"Gee, thanks." She stood gingerly and wrapped her arms around his waist. "I haven't said it yet, Drake, but thank you for coming all the way from Australia. It means a lot."

He rested his chin on top of her head and hugged her. "Of course, I came, honey. You're my family."

The nurse interrupted them with a sheaf of dismissal papers in her hand. Once that was taken care of, Ainsley had to be cajoled into a wheelchair. The woman in the blue scrubs was firm. "Hospital policy."

The older woman spent five minutes going over medication details and post-op instructions. Finally, they were allowed to leave.

Drake tucked his patient into the car with care. She seemed to be wilting already. "I'll take you home and get you settled before I go get your prescriptions," he said.

Ainsley shook her head. "That's dumb. We have to pass right by the pharmacy. I'll be fine, I swear. I might even tilt the seat back and take a nap."

Fortunately, Drake was able to get in and out of the drugstore quickly.

Ainsley didn't seem any the worse for the brief wait. When they pulled up in front of the house, she shifted in her seat. "I can't wait to see Cammie and the mystery baby," she said, her expression animated.

Drake stomach clenched. "She's excited about seeing you, too."

He gathered all Ainsley's things from the

hospital and ran them up the walk to the front porch. Then he went back to retrieve his patient. As he helped her out of the car, Ainsley batted his hands away. "I'm fine. I can do this."

"Humor me," he said, wrapping an arm around her waist as they approached the house.

The door opened before he could fish the keys out of his pocket. Cammie stood there, framed in the doorway, the baby on her hip. "Ainsley," she said, with a welcoming smile. "I'm so glad you're well enough to be home. From what Drake has told me, it must have been very scary experience."

Ainsley nodded as she entered the house. "I guess it was, but honestly, in the beginning, I was too sick to realize it."

Drake shooed the women deeper into the foyer. "Why don't you two go on into the living room and catch up? I'll carry Ainsley's things to her room."

Cammie frowned, glancing at the staircase. She addressed Ainsley. "I told Drake that the baby and I should give you the guest room, and we'll move upstairs."

Ainsley shook her head. "Thank you, but not necessary. I've been dreaming about my own room, my own bed. And the doctor says the stairs will be good exercise for me as long as I'm careful."

"Enough chitchat," Drake said, the words sharper than he intended. "You two go sit down so Ainsley can rest."

Cammie hovered until Ainsley picked a comfortable armchair. "Can I get you anything?" she asked. "A drink? Something to eat?"

The younger woman curled her legs beneath her, wincing as she moved. "No, thanks. I'm fine. They fed me before I left the hospital."

Ainsley's short, dark hair was styled in a pixie cut. With her blue eyes, she could have been blood related to Drake, though Cammie knew she wasn't. "How are you *really* feeling?" she asked. "I know Drake has probably driven you crazy hovering."

Ainsley laughed. "He does hover at times. I'm doing well," she said. "Sore and weak. But both of those conditions will get better as the days go along. It's just so good to be home. Royal Memorial is great, but I was about to go crazy."

"I'm really sorry you have to put up with houseguests. I hope it won't be much longer before Pumpkin's family is found. I suppose Drake filled you in on all the details?"

"He did." Ainsley cocked her head and stared at Cammie. "Is my stepbrother okay?" she asked. "He seems tense today."

There was nothing Cammie could do about the blush that suffused her face. "As far as I know, he's fine," she lied. "Maybe something at work is bothering him."

"I feel terrible that he dropped everything and flew all the way from Australia." Ainsley's expression was crestfallen.

"You shouldn't," Cammie said. "Drake never does anything he doesn't want to do. He loves you, and he was scared to death when he heard what happened. I think it's sweet that he takes care of you so well. Not that you're not a grown woman," she said hastily.

Drake's stepsister laughed. "You're not insulting me. He *does* take care of me. And I do appreciate it. But he has his own life, and

I have mine. I'll be fine when he goes back to Australia."

"He's leaving so soon?" Cammie felt dizzy.

"Well, not tomorrow. I know he rebooked his original flight to add a couple of days. But I told him I'll be perfectly fine on my own. Plus, I've got friends. I'm sure they wouldn't mind taking turns staying here until I'm completely back on my feet."

"Of course." Cammie swallowed. "I promise, Pumpkin and I will be out of your way in no time."

"You're not in the way." Ainsley stared at her. "So, what's going on with you and my brother? I thought the two of you broke up."

Oh, boy. Cammie wasn't prepared for the inquisition. "We did. I'm only here because I wanted to keep Pumpkin until the authorities locate his parents. I'm not qualified, but Drake is. He offered to be the official foster parent on paper. I do the actual baby care."

Ainsley chuckled. "That, I believe." She paused, clearly deciding whether or not Cammie was giving her the whole story. "Drake said he ran into you in the hospital parking lot?"

"Yes."

"That seems like a pretty big coincidence."

"Not really. I had a meeting at the hospital that day. Drake was coming to visit you. He had just flown in." Cammie started to sweat. The last thing she wanted was for Ainsley to find out that she and Drake had hooked up.

Ainsley was clearly not convinced. Cammie was forced to change the subject, but it was an awkward segue. "I haven't congratulated you on graduating from college."

"Thanks," Ainsley said. "I ended up with one of those liberal arts degrees that qualifies me for nothing in particular. But Drake says I should take my time and find a job that makes me happy."

"Don't tell him I said so," Cammie joked, "but he's a smart man."

"He is, isn't he? I'm sorry I gave him such a hard time growing up."

"You were young…and grieving. Drake understood."

"Maybe."

Cammie couldn't tell her the truth—that Drake had been indelibly marked by the conflict with his foster daughter. They related now like sister and brother. And they clearly loved each other dearly. But the harm had been done.

When Drake reappeared, ready to take Ainsley up to her room, Cammie excused herself. "It's time for this little one to eat." She avoided looking at Drake. "I'll see you both at dinner."

Before Drake could stop her, Cammie was gone. He thought he had managed to hide his frustration, but Ainsley poked him in the ribs as they walked slowly up the stairs. "What's going on with you and Cammie?"

"I don't know what you mean." The words sounded wooden even to him.

Ainsley snorted. "Oh, come on, Drake. Either you hate each other's guts, or you want to do the nasty. Which is it?"

"You're a brat," he said. "I think you need a nap."

"Denial isn't healthy, you know."

"Drop it, Ains," he said, managing not to snarl. It wasn't her fault.

She went up on her tiptoes and kissed his

cheek. "I'm sorry, Drake. You know I could go to a hotel if I'm cramping your style."

His jaw dropped. "Don't be ridiculous. You're my number one priority." He folded back the covers on her bed. "Seriously. The doctor said you need to take it easy. You don't want to end up back in the hospital."

She pouted. "You're no fun." She kicked off her shoes and climbed into bed with an audible sigh.

Drake pulled the covers up to her chin. "I want you to concentrate on getting well."

"I will." She studied his face, making him squirm inwardly. "But I need you to be happy, Drake. You gave up so much for me. You deserve to have the life you want. Or the woman…" Her arch expression finally made him smile.

"I have a great life, Ainsley. Don't you worry about me."

"I do worry. I love you. And I'm not saying that just because you're the only family I've got. You have a huge heart, but not everyone realizes that. What you did for me practically qualifies you for sainthood."

He sighed, sitting down on the edge of the

bed. "Let's not go overboard. And for the record, even though in the beginning my relationship to you felt like an obligation, you grew on me."

"Like a fungus, or maybe a rash?"

"Be serious, Ains." He paused, swallowed, and spoke gruffly. "I love you, too. You wouldn't be any more my sister if we were blood related. You know that, right?"

She was teary-eyed now. "I do. But Drake…"

He lifted an eyebrow and pinched her toe through the covers. "What?"

"Cammie is good for you. Don't let her get away again."

Ainsley's troubled gaze made him restless. His stepsister didn't know that he had basically given Cammie the boot. She would probably kick his ass if she knew.

He managed a smile. "Cammie and I are nothing now. Friends, possibly, but no romance. Maybe you're right. Maybe there's a woman out there for me."

Her face brightened. "And you swear you'll seal the deal when you find her?"

"If I find the perfect woman, you'll be the first to know."

* * *

Drake's day went from bad to worse. He hardly saw Cammie at all. She made an appearance at dinner holding the baby, but she ignored Drake for the most part, choosing instead to engage with Ainsley. He was glad to see his stepsister's face have more color and animation, but he was selfish enough to be angry when Cammie shut him out.

The three of them—four if he counted the baby—eventually moved to the living room, where the chairs were more comfortable for Ainsley. Drake had a hunch that Cammie was going to bolt at the first opportunity. But before she could hide out in the guest room, the front bell rang.

"I'll get it," Drake said.

When he opened the door, a uniformed police officer stood there. She smiled. "I'm Haley Lopez."

"I remember." Drake said. "What can I do for you?"

"May I come in and speak to you and Ms. Wentworth for a few moments?"

"Of course." He stepped back, allowing her

to enter. "Cammie and my sister, Ainsley, are in the living room."

"I hadn't heard she was released."

"Just this afternoon."

"I'm sure you're relieved."

When Drake and the officer entered the room, Cammie blanched. He introduced Haley Lopez to his stepsister. And maybe it was Drake's imagination, but he thought Cammie clutched the baby more tightly. "Have a seat," Drake said to their tall, beautiful visitor.

Cammie played with one of the baby's tiny fingers. "Do you have news, Officer Lopez?"

"Please call me Haley. Unfortunately, no. But I wanted to drop by and ask both of you a question."

Drake frowned. "We haven't heard anything, either."

"No, it's not that. Our people are still working the active investigation. But since it's taking far longer than any of us expected, social services wondered if you might like to surrender the baby to someone else in the foster parent system. I'm sure you thought this situation would resolve itself in three or four days. It's not really fair to either of you. You both have jobs and responsibilities. Ms. Conner has a family ready and willing to take Pumpkin in and care for him in the foreseeable future."

For a few moments, a long, uncomfortable silence pulsated. Even Ainsley, usually the voluble one, said nothing.

Finally, Cammie spoke. "I suppose it depends on the rules. Mr. Rhodes... Drake... will be returning to Australia in a few days. Will I be able to keep the baby if Pumpkin's official foster parent is not in the country?"

Haley frowned. "Honestly, I'm not sure. I'll have to check."

Cammie nodded. "Well, if it's possible, I'm more than willing to keep Pumpkin longer. I hate disrupting his routine."

"And I can help," Ainsley said. "I'm feeling better every day. Even with Drake gone, Cammie and I would be able to handle it."

"I'm not gone yet," Drake muttered. All three women ignored him.

Officer Lopez jotted something in her phone. "I'll explain the situation to Ms. Conner at social services. It's possible that if you two ladies are willing to continue the baby's care uninterrupted in this same home, we might be able to skate around the fact that Mr. Rhodes has to go back to Australia."

"I could change my flight," Drake said. Already, work was piling up. He was needed in Australia. On the other hand, his career wasn't brain surgery. He was free to make his own choices. And he could work remotely to some extent.

Suddenly, for the first time in hours, Cammie looked straight at him. Her gaze was cool. "You've been generous with your home and your time, Drake. I'm sure Ainsley and I can handle this. If Officer Lopez gets the situation okayed, there's no reason at all for you to change your plans. You can be on that flight to Australia in no time."

Drake was pissed. His stepsister and his former lover were basically ignoring him. Even Officer Lopez seemed to dismiss him.

Why was he feeling so rotten? Wasn't going back to Australia what he wanted? Even so, it felt damned uncomfortable to be forced out the door.

This was still his house. He would leave when he wanted to leave.

The morning after Officer Lopez's visit, Cammie fed Pumpkin, dressed both of them for the day and then tiptoed out of the bedroom. She found Mrs. Hampton in the kitchen stirring up a batch of her delicious apple muffins. After a few pleasantries, Cammie shifted the baby in her arms and said, "Am I the first one up?"

Mrs. Hampton shook her head. "Mr. Rhodes went out for an early run. Miss Ainsley is sleeping in. May I fix you something?"

Relief flooded Cammie's veins. Drake was not happy with her, so she was in no hurry to see him. "Nothing for me, thanks. I have an appointment this morning. I'll drive through somewhere on the way."

"And you're taking the baby?"

Cammie didn't know if the odd note in the housekeeper's voice indicated surprise or disapproval. "I am. It won't be a problem. If you don't mind, please tell Drake and Ainsley that I'll be back sometime this afternoon."

"Of course." The housekeeper pointed at

the nearby counter. "I still take the newspaper every day…brought my copy with me. They ran that article about your little man."

Despite the fact that Cammie was in a hurry and *really* didn't want to bump into Drake, she couldn't resist picking up the paper. She scanned the three columns. Sierra Morgan had done an excellent job. The story was compelling and heartfelt without sensationalizing Pumpkin's plight.

"It's good, isn't it?" The housekeeper shot Cammie a glance over her shoulder, waiting for an answer.

Cammie tossed the paper aside with a sigh of relief. "It is. It really is. Hopefully, we'll see progress soon."

Forty-five minutes later, she sat in a nondescript exam room and felt her heart race. This was the only time she had taken the baby out of the house and into the world. Getting him situated in the car seat hadn't been a problem. But perhaps bringing him with her had been a mistake.

This was her second recent visit to the gynecologist. The first had been for testing. Today she was going to find out the results.

When Dr. Nash walked in, Cammie took a deep breath. The other woman was in her late fifties, calm, experienced. And her manner was kind. Cammie needed that.

The ob-gyn pulled up a stool and raised an eyebrow. "Whose baby do you have?"

Cammie flushed, feeling guilty for no apparent reason. "I'm fostering him for a brief time. He was abandoned."

"Is he the one in the newspaper this morning? I read that story. Incredible that they still haven't found the parents."

"I agree. We're calling him Pumpkin. I worry that being separated from his mother at this young age may do him harm."

The doctor shook her head. "If he and his mama are reunited soon, he should be fine."

"I hope so."

The doctor carried a paper chart in her hand. She flipped it open, scanned the contents and smiled. "I'm confused," she said. "You're young. You have no apparent medical problems. You're heterosexual. Why do you want to try artificial insemination?"

Cammie clutched Pumpkin, glad to have

a shield. "I want a baby," she said, trying to sound firm.

"I understand *that*," the doctor said. "But why not do it the old-fashioned way? Wine, roses, music?"

For an instant, Cammie's memory shot back to the previous thirty-six hours…or at least the part before Ainsley came home. "I'm not in a serious relationship," she said.

The doctor's gaze was razor-sharp. "But you could be soon. What's your rush?"

It was hard to admit it, but maybe the confession would be therapeutic. "I *was* in a serious relationship," she said quietly. "Two years ago. We broke up when he found out I wanted children."

The doctor grimaced. "A lot of men think they don't want kids. They usually come around."

"Not this man," Cammie said, her throat tight. "He's adamant. And besides, our relationship ended a long time ago."

The doctor leaned back in her chair and shook her head. "I have to point out that artificial insemination comes with its own set of challenges. It's expensive, for one thing, though perhaps in your case that's not a problem. Even so, there's the issue of a sperm donor. Do you have one?"

Cammie's jaw dropped for a moment. Then she quickly snapped it shut. "I do not."

Dr. Nash sighed. "I see couples in my practice who face all manner of roadblocks on their road to conception. They are desperate. You are an anomaly, Cammie."

"So you won't help me?" Tears stung her eyes, but she didn't let them fall.

"Of course I'll help you. I'm a doctor." She reached into her pocket and handed Cammie a business card. "This is a colleague of mine. She counsels couples considering artificial insemination, particularly those who will be using a sperm donor. You might find her expertise helpful."

"I know what I want. I've always known."

"Artificial insemination is not a straightforward process. I encourage you to give this some time and thought before we talk about what comes next."

"I will." Cammie was disappointed but not dissuaded.

The doctor rolled her stool across the small

space and gathered several pamphlets from a rack on the wall. "Read through all these first. If you decide you're still interested, I have several book recommendations that go deeper into the subject. Just call my office and they can email you a list."

"But what about all my lab work?"

The doctor smiled ruefully. "By all accounts, you're extremely fertile. Getting pregnant shouldn't be any problem at all."

"Oh. That's good." Again, Cammie's thoughts flashed to Drake...the man who had been obsessively careful about using a condom. Every time. She juggled the baby and stuffed the pamphlets into her open-topped leather tote. "I'll read everything, and maybe I'll meet with your therapist person. But I don't think I'll change my mind."

"Have you considered adoption?" the doctor asked. "I included a few of those leaflets as well. There are a lot of children out there who need to be part of a family."

"I have. And I might adopt also. But first, I want to get pregnant."

"Fair enough." Dr. Nash made a notation on the chart, stood and went to the door. "See my receptionist on the way out. Schedule another appointment for two months from now. We'll talk again, Cammie."

Nine

Drake went straight to his room and showered after his run. The exercise had done little to blunt his need for Cammie, but hopefully it had given him a modicum of control. The smell of muffins drifted down the hall. A homemade breakfast and a face-to-face convo with the woman driving him crazy? He'd call that a win.

The reality wasn't exactly what he expected.

When he made it to the kitchen, only *two* women were in residence. Mrs. Hampton labored over the stove with an iron skillet. Ainsley sat at the kitchen table reading a newspaper. *A newspaper?*

Drake sat down across from his stepsister. "I didn't know anyone still published newspapers," he said, tongue firmly in cheek.

Ainsley pointed to the headline—Abandoned Baby Sparks Hunt for Mother. "This Sierra Morgan person must be the real deal. It's a great article. I like that she didn't include a picture. That might bring all the crazies out."

Drake's knee bounced under the table. He wasn't going to ask about Cammie. He wasn't. "Are you through reading that?"

She held up one finger. "Almost. Give me a sec."

Mrs. Hampton set a plate in front of him. "Eat it while it's hot," she said.

The food smelled amazing. Hickory bacon, fluffy scrambled eggs, crunchy-topped biscuits with maple butter in addition to the muffins. His mouth watered, but he couldn't bring himself to pick up his fork. He tugged at the newspaper. "You read too slow."

Ainsley surrendered the newsprint with an exaggerated sigh. "You're still a bully."

He tugged her ponytail. "And you're still a whiny baby."

His stepsister burst out laughing. "It's good to have you home, old man. It's been too quiet around here."

Don't ask about Cammie...

He cleared his throat. "How are you feeling this morning?"

"Better."

Don't ask about Cammie...

"Did you take your antibiotic?"

Her gaze narrowed. "Drake…"

He heard the message loud and clear. "Sorry," he muttered. "Old habits."

Don't ask about Cammie...

Ainsley patted his hand. "It's okay. I know you mean well." She picked up his fork and handed it to him. "Eat. Don't let the eggs get hard."

Drake made himself chew and swallow, though the food might as well have been cardboard. All he could think about was the intimate meals he and Cammie had shared recently. The way her face glowed when she looked at the baby. The way her eyes got hazy and unfocused when Drake pleasured her.

He choked on a bit of bacon and had to

wash it down with hot coffee that singed his mouth.

When Mrs. Hampton left the kitchen to take a bag of garbage outside, Ainsley frowned at him. "What's wrong with you?" she whispered. "You're weirding me out."

"Nothing's wrong," he said. "I don't know what you mean."

Suddenly, her face cleared. "Oh my gosh. It's Cammie. You're freaking out because you don't know where she is."

He went still, not looking at her. Swallowing another bite. "Do *you* know where she is?" he asked, trying for nonchalance and failing.

"Yes." Ainsley's gaze narrowed. "Mrs. Hampton said Cammie told her she had an appointment. She'll be back after lunch." Ainsley wrinkled her nose. "Damn. I guess the two of you really aren't an item. I pictured her tiptoeing down the hall to your room last night after the baby was asleep. I was hoping for big news. I always thought you two belonged together."

"There's no news," Drake said gruffly. "Let me eat my breakfast in peace."

The morning passed slowly. His office in Sydney was closed, everyone asleep. The time difference had made this trip home problematic.

Since he couldn't do business, he had plenty of time to wonder where Cammie had gone and why. And why hadn't she asked him to take care of Pumpkin while she was occupied? Didn't she trust him?

It made sense that she wouldn't ask Ainsley, who was still recovering.

Mrs. Hampton left at noon, because it was her half day. Ainsley had been on her cell phone all morning talking to friends.

Drake passed the guest suite half a dozen times before he finally entered. He stopped just inside the doorway and stared at the bed, the floor, the baby crib.

How had his orderly life been upended so completely in such a short time? He didn't like this feeling. For one thing, it was messy. He couldn't think about Cammie without thinking about the baby. The truth was, Cammie wouldn't be under his roof at all if it weren't for Pumpkin.

He told himself all he wanted was Cammie in his bed. And he was willing to tolerate the kid to make that happen. The admission painted him in an unflattering light.

Drake wasn't a bad person. He wasn't. He just didn't want to be a dad.

By one o'clock, he was pacing the floor. Ainsley was up in her room. There was no one to witness his black mood. By two o'clock, his anger morphed into worry. Cammie wasn't used to driving with a car seat in the back. What if the baby distracted her? What if she had been in an accident?

When he heard knocking and the front doorbell rang at two thirty, he was tempted to ignore it. He was in no mood for dealing with the public. But in a heartbeat, he realized that it could be someone from social services coming to check up on Pumpkin and the current home situation.

Reluctantly, he made his way down the hall. When he opened the door, shock and relief flooded his chest in equal measure. "You're back."

Cammie looked up from her purse and gave him a rueful smile. Her gorgeous red hair shone with fire in the afternoon sun and danced around her shoulders in the breeze. She tried to tuck one side behind her ear as she balanced Pumpkin on her hip, along with two medium-size shopping bags from the local market. "Sorry. I forgot to dig out my keys while I was still in the car. I decided it was easier to knock."

"No worries." He stepped back, but Cammie's shoe caught the edge of the doormat and she stumbled briefly. "Here," he said. "Give me the baby before you hurt yourself."

"Thanks." As she handed over her tiny charge, Drake's hand bumped her purse straps. Cammie's large leather tote fell off her arm and spilled all over the floor. Lip balm and papers and other feminine items scattered everywhere. When the purse fell, she lost the grocery bags, too. Baby wipes and small formula bottles added to the chaos. Fortunately, nothing broke.

"Good grief," he said. He squatted, baby in hand, and started scooping up what he could reach. Cammie did the same. He froze, his gaze incredulous, as he read the pamphlet in his hand. "You're thinking about artificial insemination? Good Lord, why?"

When he first opened the door, Cammie's expression had been carefree and happy, as if she was happy to see him. He'd felt a connection, a sexual charge. Now she was stone-faced. She finished gathering up the mess and shoved it back where it belonged. "This has nothing to do with you," she said curtly.

His temper boiled. "Ainsley!" He bellowed the summons in the general direction of the staircase.

His stepsister appeared from around the corner. She had apparently been reading in the living room, judging by the book in her hand. "You don't have to shout," she said, grimacing. "I'm right here."

"Will you watch the baby for a few minutes?" he asked. "Cammie and I need to talk. In private."

Cammie scowled. "No, we absolutely don't. And besides, Ainsley isn't supposed to exert herself."

He handed over the sleeping infant. "This nugget hardly weighs anything. Ainsley will be fine."

"I don't want to talk to you," Cammie hissed, her face flushed. Green eyes shot sparks at him.

"Too bad."

Ainsley didn't say a word, but her gaze was wide as she watched the show.

Drake took Cammie's narrow wrist in his hand and started dragging her down the hall. "Outside," he said. "Where no one can hear us."

He expected Cammie to protest, but she didn't put up a fight. At least not physically. The fact that she wasn't saying anything bugged him.

When they burst out into the sunshine, he released her. Cammie folded her arms across her chest with an *I dare you* look on her face.

"Where did you go today?" he asked. "Tell me."

Her chin went up. "To the market."

"And where else?"

"I'm not your stepsister," Cammie said. "I don't have to pay attention to your ridiculous demands."

"Cammie…" He narrowed his eyes and gave her his best intimidating glare.

She didn't seem impressed. "Why does it matter?"

He backed her up against the side of the house, into a patch of shade. Now they were standing so close, he could see the tiny pulse that fluttered at the base of her throat. "I missed you last night," he muttered.

The look in her eyes softened. "I missed you, too, Drake. But this is how it has to be. Ainsley is home, you're leaving and Pumpkin's family will be showing up any day now. Please don't make things difficult."

"I'm not sure I can do that," he said. "Kiss me, Cam."

He would have stopped, of course, if she had protested. But the way she returned the kiss so eagerly and pressed her body to his had him wondering how soon he could get her naked. He ran his hands up and down her back. "You make me burn," he said raggedly. "I can't think. I can't focus on work. I can't even remember why I'm mad at you."

She pulled back, searching his face. "Yes, you can. You saw my pamphlet from the doctor's office."

* * *

Cammie was desperate to keep herself from doing something stupid. So she threw gasoline on the fire. Mentioning the pamphlet made the situation both more and less volatile. Drake jerked back, wiping his mouth, his eyes wild.

"Tell me," he said. "Tell me what insane thing you're doing."

"Nothing's for sure yet," she said calmly. "But I want a baby, and artificial insemination is one option."

He scowled at her. "Who is he? Who's the guy donating sperm to your little experiment?"

"No one. Yet. If I decide on that choice, it will probably be someone anonymous. Entirely clinical."

"This is crazy, Cam." He ran his hands through his hair, mussing it, making him look even more appealing.

He was an incredibly beautiful man. Unfairly so. Today he was dressed very casually in jeans and a soft button-up cotton shirt in a blue that emphasized his eyes. From his broad shoulders to his masculine features and his lean frame, he was enough to make any woman's heart give a wobbly little flutter. Because he and Cammie shared a history, she was more vulnerable than most.

She shored up her resolve. "Lots of people go this route to get pregnant. Lesbian couples who want babies. Women whose partners suffer from erectile dysfunction. It's not an outlandish idea."

"But you're neither of those."

"True," she said. "I don't have a partner at all."

She saw him flinch. Perhaps she had wounded his pride, but she was tired of pretending. "I've been thinking about this for months. *You* want to build a business empire. I want to create a family. It's my choice."

He came back to her then, suddenly looking as dangerous as a tiger on the prowl. "Let me give you my sperm," he said. "I don't like the idea of some strange man fathering your child. It's creepy."

"It's *not* creepy. And do you know how ridiculous you sound? No way. You'd never be able to forget that you had a son or daughter walking around Royal."

A shadow crossed his face. For a moment, she saw true vulnerability in his masculine gaze. The glimpse was so shocking she barely knew how to react. Drake Rhodes was an alpha male to the core. He knew what he wanted, and he went after it. Be it business or pleasure, he was the commander of his own destiny. Confident, arrogant. Entirely sure of himself and his decisions.

Often, Cammie had envied his certainty. Her life had never been so clear-cut.

"I have to go in," she said, feeling suddenly exhausted.

"Not yet, Cam." He pulled her into his arms a second time and kissed her lazily. His lips were firm and warm on hers. His arms folded her close, creating a haven of safety and security that was as arousing as it was wonderful. When he set his mind to it, Drake could make a mockery of her resolve. She loved him dearly. Far too much to resist. He wasn't even gone yet, and already she was grieving his loss.

When he slid one big, warm hand under the skirt of her sundress and found her center, she groaned. He stroked her through thin panties, raising her temperature and fracturing her breathing.

Longing, hot and fierce, writhed in her core. "Please," she begged. "Please." Not even sure what she was asking for, she burrowed closer, her cheek pressed to his chest. She felt his lips in her hair.

"Come for me, Cam," he muttered. "Come, my love."

Those last two words hurt, uttered as they were in the pursuit of carnal pleasure. But even knowing the falseness of his ragged demand, she couldn't help herself. She hit the peak, sobbing, drowning in the hot, sweet pleasure.

He held her close as she drifted back to earth. She felt his hand on the back of her head, his fingers combing her sun-warmed hair. Words trembled on her tongue, but she couldn't give them voice. She couldn't beg him to be someone he wasn't.

His voice was low and gravelly when he spoke. "We'll meet in my room tonight, Cam. Please. I understand all the problems. But I don't care. Do you?"

She did—she cared a lot. But he was right.

Even knowing the pain that lay ahead, she wanted him. "I'll come," she said. "But we mustn't let Ainsley know. This is her home. You are her family. We'll spend the day and the evening with her."

Drake rested his forehead against hers. "I love your tender heart and the way you care about people."

His words were complimentary, but they cut like knives. He hadn't said he loved *her*. That was a huge difference. "Thank you, Drake." She stepped away and smoother her hair. "The baby will be hungry. I need to tend to him."

"You won't change your mind?"

His intensity both thrilled and pained her. Drake wanted her badly. But only her body. Only that. Not her future. She swallowed against the bitter taste of regret. "I won't change my mind," she said.

As Cammie sat in the rocker in her room and fed the baby his bottle, her thoughts wandered. The doctor's words disturbed her. Why did she need to see a counselor? She knew her own mind. Wanting a baby was nothing new.

She craved that connection, that opportunity to build a family. Though it might not seem so to an outsider, Cammie was alone in the world. Her father was wrapped up in his own interests. Even with the Danae Foundation and his new bent toward philanthropy, he still had little warmth to offer his daughter.

Rafe Wentworth was a brother in absentia, a sibling on paper only. He, too, lived his own life. And Cammie's relationship with her mother had been strained after her father's first divorce years ago.

If anything, Drake was the one person who had shown her what it was like to be cherished and cared for. Even though he had never said the words, and even though she knew his feelings for her were more affection than real love, Drake had supported her, spent time with her and gone out of his way to make her happy. Right up until the day he couldn't do it anymore.

Her desire to get pregnant had been a line in the sand he couldn't cross.

Later that evening, the four of them sat at the dinner table. Ainsley, clearly feeling better, chattered away. She and Drake were discussing an internship she'd been offered beginning in the new year.

Cammie held Pumpkin and ate her dinner, content to let the conversation wash over her. Mrs. Hampton had left a homemade lasagna for the evening meal. Drake and Ainsley heated bread and put together a salad. The meal was delicious, but it was the bubble of contentment that fed Cammie's soul.

This was what she wanted, what she had always wanted.

Ainsley inadvertently broke Cammie's warm, fuzzy mood when she questioned her stepbrother. "So be honest, Drake. When *is* your flight back to Sydney? I'll be fine. But I don't like surprises."

Join the club, Cammie thought wryly.

Drake looked as if he had swallowed a bad piece of cheese. "Um…" His face flushed. "It's scheduled for day after tomorrow, but I think I'll bump it two more days. Just to be safe. I want to make sure you're on the mend, and I wouldn't mind seeing Pumpkin reunited with his family. I'd hate for all that to go down after I leave."

The shock literally stole the breath from

Cammie's lungs. The pain cut through her body without mercy. How she managed not to respond visibly was a mystery.

Inside, she cried. She had known he was leaving soon. But to hear him say it on the heels of their plan to be intimate tonight seemed...well, cruel.

He shot a glance in her direction, clearly trying to gauge her mood. Cammie would be damned before she would give him the satisfaction. Her smile was bland. "You'll spend a lot of money on flight changes."

Drake shrugged. "Such is life. My crew in Sydney knows my plans are fluid. They want me back, but they'll juggle things in the meantime."

"Well, I'm glad you have staff you can rely on," Ainsley said. "I feel guilty enough about upending your work schedule. And there's no need to add those two extra days. I'm feeling great."

Cammie was pretty sure that *great* was an exaggeration. But it wasn't her place to interfere between the other two. That was a relationship with its own dynamic. She had enough worries of her own.

When she finally made it back to her room to put the baby down for the night, she closed the door to the hall and sagged against it. Tears leaked down her cheeks. Her knees were weak, and her head pounded. The two hours of pretending to socialize normally had required every ounce of her acting ability.

Forty-eight hours. Drake could be gone in forty-eight hours. Maybe ninety-six if he did what he said and tacked on two more days. Honestly, she hoped he didn't do that.

Why torture herself? Maybe Pumpkin's mother would be located overnight, and Cammie would be free.

She went through the motions with Pumpkin and then realized what she was doing. This was dumb. The baby shouldn't suffer because of Cammie's heartache. After she bathed him, she put on his diaper and picked her favorite sleeper to dress him.

Afterward, she fed him and walked the floor, choosing to sing instead of rocking him. She had read that babies needed to learn to self-soothe and fall asleep naturally, but surely not in this case. An innocent infant had lost his mama.

It was nine thirty when his little head lolled on her shoulder. They had fallen into a pattern of sorts. Pumpkin would probably sleep until two or three.

Cammie took a quick shower. She had ordered a soft negligee and robe to wear now that Ainsley was home. It had been delivered this morning. She clipped off the tags and slid the softy silky gown over her damp body.

Would Drake like the way she looked?

And did it matter?

She picked up her phone and sent him a text.

Is Ainsley upstairs for the night?

Drake's answer was immediate. Yes. I'm waiting for you.

Cammie could almost feel his impatience in those five words. She grabbed the baby monitor, took a deep breath to steady her nerves and opened her door.

This was the end. She felt it in her bones and made peace with the bitter knowledge. After all, this whole interlude with Drake had been nothing but happenstance. An abandoned baby. A chance encounter in a parking lot. A man juggling guilt and duty.

She would take this one final night greedily. Because she was too weak to deny him and herself. If this was all she would ever have of Drake Rhodes, the memories would have to last her a lifetime.

Ten

Drake was buzzing with nerves and caffeine. Earlier, Ainsley had admitted to overdoing things today. She had bid him good night and gone upstairs at eight.

He had been left to walk the floors and wonder when—or if—Cammie would come to him.

It would have helped if he could have gone for another run, but he was afraid to leave on the off chance Cammie would seek him out and he'd be gone.

At nine he locked the doors and turned out the lights—all except the one in the hallway between his room and Cammie's. After that, he showered. Then he paced his bedroom. It was a large space, but not large enough.

He knew he had emails waiting. The office in Australia was open now. But for the first time in months, he couldn't focus. Nor could he summon up any particular interest in his business affairs.

All he could think about was Cammie.

How could she even contemplate becoming a single parent? Didn't she know how hard that would be? How lonely?

His brain shied away from the idea of his Cammie going to a sperm bank and selecting a donor. That process was too impersonal.

Hell, Drake didn't want to become a dad, but even he knew the process would be easier if he and Cammie were in bed together.

In the midst of his tortured thoughts, Cammie opened the door and walked right in. She didn't even knock. When he saw what she was wearing, his tongue felt thick in his mouth. He blinked and searched for words.

"Finally," he said. *Oops. That came out wrong.* He didn't want to sound critical. "I'm glad to see you."

Her small, mocking smile said she recognized his clumsy lack of savoir faire. "I told you I would come."

"What happened to the football jersey?" he asked. "I liked it."

The gown she wore was coffee-colored silk trimmed in cream lace. It was cut low between her breasts in front. When she shimmied out of the matching robe and tossed it on his chair, he saw that the V on the back of the gown went even lower. It revealed the faintest hint of her ass. The fabric skimmed her curves, tantalizing…seductive.

Hell, Drake didn't need to be seduced. Arousal pulsed through his veins and hardened his body. He wanted to snatch and devour. It would be difficult to offer her tenderness, but shouldn't he try?

He reached out and turned off the lights. Now only a single candle burned. It was his one attempt at romance.

There was no shyness about Cammie's posture, no tentative nerves. She came right up to him and put her hands on his shoulders. Her smile was both sweet and challenging. If there were shadows in her gaze, he couldn't see them.

She went up on her tiptoes and kissed his lips softly. Her body nestled against his. "Let's not waste any time."

Curiously, her willingness to jump right in made it easier to keep his vow. "Patience, Cammie." He scooped her up in his arms, feeling the erotic slide of silk beneath his fingertips as he held her. Her hair trailed over his elbow. Bending his head, he nuzzled her cheek. "You look amazing. Too bad I can't let you wear that gorgeous thing in bed."

Her grin was impish. "Can't? Or won't? I spent a lot of money on this."

He dropped her carefully on the mattress. Earlier, he had turned back the sheets and covers. "It was worth every penny," he said, "but I want you naked while I do naughty things to your delectable body."

Her eyes rounded. "I don't know whether I should be excited or scared."

Drake laughed. He ditched his boxers and joined her. "Why not both?" When his body twined with hers, he had to take a jerky breath. He was playing a dangerous game. Both with Cammie and with his own life.

This need he felt should have been simple.

Sleep with an old lover. Friends with benefits. Carpe diem.

Instead, he felt like he was drowning. The
pleasure was both wonderful and terrifying.
He had to get on a plane. Soon. Or he might
do something that would change his life ir-
revocably. Being a good guy seven years ago
had altered his entire world. He couldn't do
it again. He knew his own limitations.

To silence the annoying voice in his head,
he kissed Cammie. She murmured something
low in her throat, a feminine sound that made
the hair on his arms stand up. Hearing her
pleasure and knowing that he was the one
making her purr elated him.

He took the kiss deeper still. Though he had
threatened to strip her naked, now he paused
to enjoy the feel of her hips and her breasts
and the dip of her waist, all of it packaged in
warm, silky fabric that beckoned his touch.

Their tongues tangled lazily. He knew her
taste intimately. When she nipped his bottom
lip with sharp teeth, he was shocked. Cammie was rarely the aggressor in their love
play. What was different about her tonight?

Perhaps, like Drake himself, she was trying

to squeeze every last drop of carnal pleasure from their last time together. Or was it? He hadn't changed the airline ticket yet. Either way, he felt stuck. Change it—and miss time with Cammie…and Ainsley. Extend it—and get drawn more deeply into a domestic scenario with long tentacles.

Cammie slid her arms around his neck. When she played with his earlobes, his erection lengthened. He sucked in an audible breath.

His lover chuckled. "I love the way your body responds to my touch, Drake. You make a woman feel powerful."

"You *are* powerful, Cam. I'm surprised you don't know that."

His answer seemed to surprise her. The smile disappeared. She searched his face as if he were a puzzle she was trying to solve.

There was no puzzle. He wanted Cammie Wentworth. Always had. And he wanted to make her happy. But that last part was out of his control.

"I think it's time for you to be naked," he said huskily. "Sit up for me."

He shimmied the gown up to her hips as she moved. Then, when she lifted her arms, he pulled the silk and lace over her head and tossed it to the foot of the bed. As he cupped her full breasts in his palms, her eyes closed, and her head fell back.

All Drake could do was wallow in the moment. She was here. In his bed. It was a bit of a miracle. The situation had him feeling rash and impetuous. When he thumbed her soft pink nipples, Cammie muttered his name.

"Drake," she whispered. "Drake."

The yearning in those syllables was impossible to miss. "I'm here, sweetheart. I'm here." He eased her onto her back and slid down beside her.

When he spread her thighs and tried to move on top of her, her eyes flew open in alarm. She put a hand to his chest. "The condom," she said urgently.

Everything inside him pushed toward the goal. Maybe he could be a hero after all. He slid two fingers inside her, feeling how ready she was. Noting how her body wanted his. "Let me give you a baby, Cam," he said urgently. "The old-fashioned way. I'll sign my rights away. I won't interfere. But you'll have that family you've always wanted."

Her gaze went wide and dark, the irises almost swallowed up by her pupils. A single tear squeezed from the corner of her eye and trickled down her flushed cheek. Cammie didn't seem to notice.

She caught his face in her hands, her expression wistful and tender. "That's a lovely offer, Drake. And I do appreciate it. But I can't accept. You would come to regret your decision and to resent me. I can't risk that."

"I wouldn't," he said, but the words lacked conviction, even to his own ears. He wanted to give her the moon and stars and everything in between. But if she wouldn't take his gift, was he any use to her at all?

Cammie pulled his face down for a kiss. Then she ran her hands down his back and cupped his flanks. "Get the protection, my sexy man."

Balanced as he was on his hands, her exploration of his body made his arms weak even as the rest of him pulsed with power and resolve. He was pissed on some level that she was rejecting his very generous offer. But he was too hungry to let a disagreement—even such an important one—derail the moment.

Feeling disgruntled and frustrated, he reached for the packet on the bedside table, took care of business and came back to her. Once again, he tried for tenderness. But he was too far gone, pushed perhaps by the thought he couldn't get out of his head. Cammie, pregnant and lovely, but with a child that wasn't his.

He shut his mind to the images, concentrating instead on the living, breathing woman in his bed. "I need you, Cam. Hard and fast. It's been too long."

"Ainsley's barely been home," she reminded him.

"I don't care. It feels like forever."

He entered her slowly, lifting one of her legs and propping it on his shoulder so he could go deep.

Cammie's gasp reflected what he was feeling. This was as close to heaven as a guy like him could get. The visual was incredible, but no more so than the feel of burying his aching sex inside Cammie. Her body welcomed him, gripped him, made his brow break out in a sweat. "Damn, woman," he croaked. "What are you doing to me?"

After that, he could no longer think. Cammie lifted into his thrusts. When she wrapped her free leg around his waist, his vision blurred. He needed her so badly, he couldn't breathe. His chest labored for oxygen.

He took her again and again, desperate to find what he was seeking. Dimly, he heard Cam cry out as she climaxed. But he wasn't done. He held back, reining in his own need, bent on proving something to someone.

But in the end, he was mortal. Flawed. Just a man. His orgasm ripped through him from his feet to his hair follicles and everywhere in between. He shouted at the very end, muffling the noise against her shoulder.

Cammie held him as he shuddered in her embrace. He felt her fingers in his hair. In despair, he recognized at that moment that he loved her. But it changed nothing. He was getting on a plane to Australia. Whatever Cammie decided about motherhood would have nothing at all to do with him...

* * *

After Drake fell asleep, Cammie contemplated the seismic carnage. Drake had been like a madman. The covers were tumbled and beyond reach of her numb fingers. Now that the fierce coupling was over, her heated skin cooled.

Her lover was a dead weight, pressing her into the bed.

She could have moved him, but that required more effort than she could summon at the moment. The encounter had stunned her.

From the first time she and Drake had become lovers several years ago, there had always been something powerful that happened when they were together in a sexual encounter. She had been fairly inexperienced, so she always assumed that he was simply a very good lover.

But it was more than that.

Now, with the distance of time—and their recent reunion—she understood that they were made for each other; physically, that was. A very strong attraction had survived two years apart and even Drake's stint in Australia.

Why else had she gone back to his bed so quickly? It was almost as if no time had passed at all. What she felt for him was not going to change. Maybe that's why she needed to talk to a counselor.

The memory of Drake's offer to give her a baby made her eyes sting with emotion. In other circumstances, she would have been elated. But he wasn't having a change of heart about becoming a father. He didn't want to build a family and a lifetime with her. He was literally offering his DNA.

If he but knew, that was absolutely the *worst* idea. For Cammie to have a son or daughter with Drake's deep blue eyes and wavy black hair would be too painful to imagine. She would never be able to escape his presence.

She knew his gesture meant he cared about her. A lot. And that was comforting. But in the end, what Drake wanted from life was not what Cammie could offer him. He wanted to be free.

The baby monitor rested across the room on a small table. At this particular moment, it would have been nice for Cammie to have an excuse to leave. Beneath her fingertips,

Drake's skin didn't feel cold at all. How was that possible? Evidently, the life force he wielded was too strong to allow something as simple as a chilly room to affect him.

She kissed his shoulder lightly and prepared to nudge him over onto his side of the bed. When she tried, he roused groggily. "Is it the baby?" he asked.

"No." She slipped from his arms. "I'm going to the bathroom."

Drake was asleep again before she had taken three steps.

In the mirror over the vanity, Cammie studied her reflection. Her warring emotions were right there on her face for anyone to see. First was the smug happiness of a woman who had been well loved. Physical satisfaction. Sexual satiation.

But even in the midst of her momentary bliss, her eyes held sadness. A bleak certainty that Drake wasn't hers. The breakup from two years ago was still intact. Even though she and Drake had used living under the same roof as an excuse to revisit their physical relationship, nothing else had changed.

She was too tired to shower again. Instead, she wet a washcloth and found some of Drake's expensive shower gel to freshen up. There was nothing she could do about the hickey at her collarbone or the red patches on her throat where Drake's late-night stubble had scratched her.

Everything about her body felt his imprint.

When she returned to the bedroom, the candle burned low. Drake was on his stomach now, with both arms flung over his head. The sheet had crumpled down around his feet. For one private moment, she stood there and admired the picture he made.

An artist might have titled it *Masculine Excess*.

When her skin pebbled with goose bumps, she reached for her gown and robe and put them on, tying the sash at her waist. The lovely lingerie made her feel feminine and sexy, but it was the man in the bed who made her feel desirable and whole.

Leaving him was hard.

She sat down on the side of the bed and touched his warm shoulder, her fingers lingering to stroke and pet. "Drake."

It took him a few seconds to wake up. He

rubbed the heels of his hands in his eyes. "What are you doing?"

"I'm heading back to my room," she said simply. She leaned down and kissed his warm, firm lips, lingering over the caress when he curled an arm around her waist and wouldn't let her move.

"Don't go," he said, the words ragged and hoarse.

She sat up, despite his efforts to constrain her. "It's for the best. Pumpkin will be awake soon."

"But not yet." He wrapped his fingers around her nearest wrist.

"I'm tired," she said simply. "This was wonderful, but I desperately need to get some sleep. I'll see you in the morning."

He sat up abruptly, seeming unconcerned with his spectacular nudity. "I'll be gone," he said, yawning.

Her heart fell to her feet. She felt sick and dazed. "Gone? I thought your flight was the next day."

In the midst of her internal meltdown, Drake continued to speak. "Not that kind of gone. I have an early doctor's appointment."

She pulled the sheet to his waist, trying to protect her flimsy self-control.

Since the man was the picture of health, she wasn't *too* concerned. But still she had to ask. "Are you okay?"

He smiled and rubbed his thumb over her cheek. "I'm great. It's just a technical thing. Ainsley is the beneficiary on my life insurance policy. Now that I'm living part of the year in Australia, my current company doesn't want to cover me. The new guys require a physical. Since I was here in Royal, I simply made an appointment with my own doctor. It shouldn't take long."

"Ah..." The relief she felt was way out of proportion to the actual situation.

"And do me a favor," he said with a rueful smile. "Please don't mention it to Ainsley. She gets squirrelly when we talk about it. So I don't bring it up."

"Of course." Cammie forced herself to stand, though it was the last thing she wanted to do. "Good night, Drake."

He rolled out of bed and stood as well, cupping her head in his hands, winnowing his fingers through her hair. "Pumpkin is on my side tonight," he said. "Still snoozing." The words were joking, but his gaze was dead serious. "I'm leaving, Cam. Don't cheat us of the time we have left."

You're the one cheating us...

Cammie wanted to yell at him, cajole him, do everything in her power to change the man he was. But if she did that, he wouldn't be the Drake she fell in love with. He had made up his mind. End of story.

Though bitterness tried to take hold, Drake's touch was stronger. "Okay," she said. The word threatened to stick in her throat.

His hands went to the knot at the front of her robe. "Don't be sad, Cammie. I don't want that for you. You should have everything you desire."

Hurt bubbled in her chest. His words were facile, totally ignoring the heart of the matter. How could he say that and not realize he was the problem?

As Drake undressed her and carried her back to the bed, she leaned her head against his chest. From out of nowhere, a thought struck her. Maybe she was as stubborn as Drake. Maybe she had been heaping all the blame for her unhappiness on him unfairly. Maybe she was equally culpable.

This time, Drake didn't rush. The foreplay was slow as molasses. He touched her everywhere, whispering words of praise, telling her all the ways her body pleased him and all the ways he wanted to return that pleasure tenfold.

She wallowed in the tenderness, all the while anticipating the moment when his hunger would overtake this infinitely precious *play*. He looked younger now, more relaxed, sweet and diabolically teasing.

Despite her fatigue and the late hour, he coaxed her latent desire to the surface.

What would happen if she abandoned her plans to have a baby? Had Drake used her desire for motherhood as an excuse to get out of a permanent relationship? Or was there a possibility that he cared a fraction as much as she did?

As he kissed his way from her throat to her navel, she dizzily pondered her revelation. Would he want permanence if parenthood was out of the question? If so, maybe she could have this bliss every night forever.

Drake was a wonderful man. Funny and charming. Intelligent and driven. They could have an amazing life together. Travel. See the world. And Cammie could even run the Danae Foundation from a distance, given technology in the twenty-first century.

Lots of people lived full and amazing lives without children.

She had spent so long being absolutely sure that she *had* to have a baby. Could she change? Could she take a step back and pivot? There were dozens of ways to help children in Royal and around the world. Funding important projects. Donating volunteer hours. The possibilities were endless.

Perhaps it was the late hour. Perhaps she was light-headed from getting no sleep. But a flicker of hope refused to die.

Still, every time she tried to imagine being childless for the rest of her life, her heart shied away from the thought.

Equally terrible was the very real notion of Drake flying away from Royal and never coming back for anything but fleeting visits.

She loved him. Could she give up her dream for him?

And if she gave up that dream, did Drake love her in return?

He kissed her then, long and deep. Rational thought evaporated. "Drake," she whispered. "Drake…"

Rolling her onto her side, he spooned her and entered her from behind, with her leg over his. This position, though she could no longer see his face, was oddly intimate. He cradled her in his arms, keeping the pace languid.

As he played with her breasts and thrust slowly, she felt tears sting her eyes. What they had was so precious. Couldn't he see that? And seeing it, want to pass it on to another generation?

Her heart was breaking even as Drake stroked her body with his sex and his hands and brought her to a shivering climax. He was seconds behind her, burying his face in her nape as he groaned and found release.

They dozed after that. Pumpkin slept on.

When Cammie finally heard baby sounds on the monitor, thirty minutes had passed.

Groggy and weighed down with uncertainty, she found her nightwear, dressed and hurried down the hall. When she picked up the baby and felt his warmth and weight against her breast, she wanted to howl with frustration and despair.

Already she loved this *borrowed* baby deeply. How much more would she love her own son or daughter? Born of her body or adopted from her heart. Either way, she would give a child all the love and attention and *normalcy* she had missed growing up.

The routines of diaper and feeding were second nature to her now. She rocked Pumpkin, watching for the first faint rays of dawn to sneak around the heavy, expensive drapes. The day would begin whether she wanted it to or not.

The hours would tick by.

Drake's departure would draw near.

Had this small, unknown baby come into their lives to work a miracle, or was all of it a coincidence?

Cammie didn't really believe in fate. But right now, she wouldn't mind a glimpse into the future. So much to gain. So much to lose. And an hourglass where the sand was disappearing far too quickly.

Eleven

Drake didn't see Cammie before he left the house. She was either avoiding him, or the baby had gone back to sleep and Cammie was resting, too.

He was glad, in a way. Last night was etched into his memory. His body felt achy and relaxed at the same time. Sexually speaking, it had been one of the best nights of his life.

Why, then, was he feeling oddly out of sorts this morning?

He had allowed himself plenty of extra time to do a few errands en route to the doctor's office. Which was a good thing, because his Realtor called while he was on the way. Her voice was noticeably excited when she said hello.

"What's up?" he asked, searching for a parking spot on the street. There was never anything in the multilevel garage.

The agent gushed. "You're never going to believe it, Drake. We've had a cash offer on the ranch. Ten percent over asking price."

The bottom fell out of his stomach. "I see." He put the vehicle in Park and shut it off. Gripping the wheel with both hands, he tried to think of what to say.

His silence obviously confused his caller. "I thought you'd be pleased," she said.

Instead of responding to that comment, he cleared his throat. "How long do I have to think about it?"

"Are you kidding me?" The incredulity in her voice said she was already spending the hefty commission.

"I never actually listed the ranch," he said.

"But you let someone look at it." The retort was sharp and probably well deserved.

"I told you I was conflicted about selling. You were the one who pushed me. I thought the whole thing was pretty casual and unofficial. We never signed stuff."

He had her there. But she was good at her job. She changed tack. "I know this is a hard decision. It would be for anybody. You love the ranch. But you don't even live in Royal anymore, Drake. Don't let sentimentality get in the way of a sound business decision."

Again, he asked, "How long do I have to give them an answer?"

Her silence was longer this time. He fancied he could hear her disgust over the phone line. "Forty-eight hours," she said with a long-suffering sigh. "And they'd like to close in two weeks."

Twenty minutes later—in the physician's waiting room—Drake stewed. Decisions were coming at him hard and fast. Tomorrow he was supposed to board a flight to Sydney. He'd just had a text from Cammie telling him that social services approved Pumpkin's care with Cammie and Ainsley as long as they stayed in the same house.

So Drake could leave tomorrow with no qualms, no guilt.

He grimaced, feeling as if his entire life in

Royal was being stripped away all at once. He loved this town, loved the life he had known here. And as much as he might try to deny it, he loved Cammie Wentworth. So why then was he walking out the door?

When the nurse called him back and checked his vitals, she raised an eyebrow. "Your blood pressure is up. Not bad, but unusual for you."

"I had a phone call right before I came in," he said, shrugging.

"I hope not bad news."

The woman was making small talk. Being polite. But Drake answered anyway. "Just one of those fork-in-the-road things," he said ruefully.

She made a couple of entries on his electronic chart. "I understand. Stress can make the BP go up. But you're here for an insurance physical, so we'll let the doctor check it again before you go."

Drake had come by for blood work a few days ago. Today was only a formality. He would hear the results and get the forms signed. He concentrated on deep breathing. The last thing he wanted was to get turned down by this company, too. He was healthy as a horse. All he needed was to protect Ainsley's future.

Like in most medical establishments, Drake had to wait. It made him antsy, but he checked email and tried to stay calm so his BP would hit the normal range.

When the door finally opened, Dr. Brad Stockton walked into the room. He shook Drake's hand. "Good to see you, Drake."

"You, too." He and the doc had known each other since they were kids. "So, any surprises in the bloodwork? Your nurse said my blood pressure was a little high today. I told her I was stressed."

Brad grabbed a cuff and wrapped it around Drake's arm. "We're all stressed, aren't we? We live with it." He pumped and listened. Finally, he unwound the cuff and set it aside. "You're in the normal range. Barely. Nothing to cause problems with the insurance stuff. But it's my job to tell you to chill out. Find a hobby. Take some time off."

Drake managed a smile, thinking about his erotic overnight activities. You'd think that would count for something. "Duly noted," he said. "Are you signing off on everything else? I need to get this policy in place ASAP."

"Because you're heading back to Australia?"

"Yep." The word stuck in his throat.

The doctor pulled up a stool and sat at the computer. "Whenever I do these insurance physicals, I always check for any red flags that might derail things. In your case, of course, you're young and healthy. So I don't see any problems."

"But?" He could tell Brad was headed somewhere.

His childhood playmate turned around with a grimace. "You know we have access now to electronic pharmacy records."

"Yes." Drake frowned. Had there been some kind of mix-up?

The other man put his elbows on his knees and leaned forward. "Tell me something about your time in Australia. I saw that you were on an antibiotic and steroids."

Drake sighed, relieved. "Oh, yeah. That was several months ago. I was snorkeling off one of the beaches south of Melbourne and cut my leg on some coral. I didn't go to the doctor right away, and it got infected. But no worries. It cleared up beautifully." He pulled up his pants leg, pointing to his shin. "The scar isn't bad at all."

Brad looked closely at the pinkish streak, poked at it carefully and nodded. "That does look good."

"Then why do I get the feeling you're about to tell me something bad?"

"Not bad," the doctor said. "Not necessarily. But the antibiotic they gave you is a very strong one. And you were on it for four weeks. I'm sure they were concerned the infection might spread. Who knows what was in that ocean water? That particular medication is one we don't use much here."

"They told me they wanted to be very careful, because they'd had several cases of flesh-eating bacteria."

"Ah…"

Drake frowned. "But I'm not in any danger now, am I?"

"No. Not at all. It's just that a powerful antibiotic like the one you took can cause male infertility."

Was it Drake's imagination, or did the

room shrink and go oddly silent? So what? He didn't want kids. This wasn't bad news, was it?

Brad was a trained professional. He couldn't have missed Drake's shock. "Don't jump ahead on this," he said, his expression kind. "If you and your partner decide to try for a baby, all I'm telling you is that it would be smart to see a specialist beforehand. That way you'll know in advance if you're dealing with any issues."

"Thanks," Drake said. He could barely get the word out.

Fifteen minutes later, he was out on the street, his world turned upside down. He knew he was in shock. His ears were ringing, and he had a hard time unlocking his car.

He couldn't go home not yet. So he drove out to the ranch.

Why had he let anyone think the ranch was up for sale? As he headed past the open gates and down the winding gravel road, several longtime employees who recognized him lifted a hand.

Drake waved back, though he felt anything but carefree. Normally, being here soothed him, pleased him. He'd grown up on this property.

Though he could have stopped at the comfortable and luxurious ranch house, he drove on, deeper and deeper into the massive acreage he owned. Finally, several miles from the main hub of activity, he scaled a low hill, parked the car and got out. A small cottonwood tree offered a patch of shade. Even though the rise was modest, the surrounding land was flat. He could see a very long way.

What he couldn't see was the image of his own future.

The doctor's cautionary advice had been a dash of icy water in Drake's face. Only when he heard the word *infertility* did he realize that his subconscious had been hard at work spinning various scenarios where Drake could keep Cammie in his life and still maintain the status quo.

He'd come up with several ideas. The easiest one was to take her to Australia with him and persuade her to give up on the idea of getting pregnant. But even in his most optimistic moments, he had known that was unlikely.

What he hadn't realized until this very instant was that he'd also been weaving another tale. The one where he took Cammie to Australia with him, but then promised to come back to Royal and start a family.

When had he begun to release his stubborn, long-held ban on babies? Was it the day he rushed home to Ainsley's bedside, knowing how much their bond meant to him? Or when he came face-to-face with Cammie and the abandoned child?

More likely, it had been in the midst of incredible sex. When he had known without a doubt that if he didn't change his mind, he risked losing the only woman who had made him feel invincible.

Though he hadn't changed his flight for tomorrow, deep in his gut, he knew he shouldn't get on that plane without resolving something with Cammie. He loved her. Maybe he had always loved her. During his time in New York, he had come back to Royal frequently.

The months in Australia had a been a different proposition. Royal had seemed very far away. But at night—even on the far side of the globe—he still dreamed of Cam occasionally. His professional life had been going smoothly, but he never felt entirely settled in Sydney. There was always something missing.

Now, he knew the *something* was a *someone*. Cammie.

All along, ever since he had jumped in to take responsibility for the abandoned child and made sure to keep Cammie under his roof and in his bed, his innermost self had been adjusting, growing, seeking new answers.

Some tiny part of him had come to believe that giving Cammie a baby wouldn't be such a bad thing at all.

He had let the idea simmer, occasionally poking at it, studying it, wondering if he really had the mental fortitude to be a dad, this time from the very beginning.

But what now? Even if he told her he loved her, it wouldn't be enough. To say those words to her, knowing what he now knew, meant possibly breaking her heart all over again. What if he couldn't get her pregnant? What then?

Because he couldn't go home, he slid down

to the ground and rested his back against the tree. What in the hell was he going to do?

Cammie and Ainsley had a wonderful morning with Pumpkin. Ainsley even took charge of him for half an hour so Cammie could take a nap. When Cammie stumbled back into the living room and fell into a chair, yawning, Ainsley stared at her in concern.

"Are you okay?" she asked, clearly noting the dark circles under Cammie's eyes.

"I didn't sleep well last night," Cammie admitted.

"Why?"

Lying was not Cammie's strong suit, so she told a half-truth. "I was worried about the baby. About how much longer it will be before they finally locate his family. It shouldn't be like this."

"You love him, don't you?" the younger woman said, her blue-eyed gaze filled with sympathy.

Cammie shrugged, feeling weepy but trying to pull herself together. "How could I not? Honestly, when I brought him here, I thought it would be twenty-four or forty-eight hours at most. Now I've had time to really get to know him. He's so small, but he has his definite likes and dislikes."

"Just like a man," Ainsley said, grinning.

"Do *you* ever think about having children?"

Ainsley rubbed the baby's head, her expression reflective. "Occasionally. But I'm only twenty-two. I've got time."

"Will you tell me about you and Drake?" Cammie asked. "He never really talked much to me about your shared past."

"The man doesn't like to reveal his emotions, you know."

"I do know," Cammie said.

Ainsley put the baby on his back in her lap and let him curl his tiny fingers around her pinkies. "Drake's mom died young of cancer."

"Yes."

"And my dad died of a heart attack when I was thirteen. Even now, my hazy memories tell me that Mom wasn't too sad he was gone. From what she said over the years, he was a very hard man to be married to…maybe even abusive, though I hope not. Anyway, my mom didn't stay single long. She'd only been a widow a year, and then boom…she was getting married to Drake's dad."

"Did you all live at the ranch?"

"Yes, though Drake was away at college most of the time," Cammie said. "When our parents were killed in the car accident, suddenly, I was alone."

"You and Drake both…"

"I suppose that's true. But he was the same age I am now. He could handle himself."

Cammie pushed, feeling protective of the man she loved. "Still, it was traumatic for him, too."

"Of course," Ainsley said. "I didn't mean to imply it wasn't. But no one was going to send him off to strangers. I know most foster parents are wonderful. But I had heard stories, and I was terrified."

"How soon did you know what Drake was going to do?"

"Almost right away. After the funeral, we were both sitting in the kitchen at the ranch. The house was quiet. No one was around. Suddenly he told me he would get licensed as a foster parent so that I could stay with him."

"What did you think of the idea?" Cammie asked.

"At first I was glad, but soon he started acting like a real parent, and I resented that. I resented *him*. I was a total pain in the ass, Cammie. I've heard him say he doesn't want kids because of what he went through with me. He makes it sound like a joke, but I know it's true. I made his life hell for several years. You don't know how much I regret that."

Cammie didn't know how to respond to the raw, pained confession. "Well," she said slowly. "It was a long time ago. And you have a great relationship now. That should count for something."

"Maybe. I don't know. Sometimes I think I broke him." Her comical face punctuated the half-serious statement.

Cammie laughed, as Ainsley intended. "You didn't break him. Drake is fine. He has a great life and a challenging, exciting job. But tell me, why didn't you and he continue living at the ranch?"

Ainsley sighed. "I think it was just too damn sad with his dad and my mom gone. Drake offered to buy a house in town so I would be closer to school, and I said yes. We've been here ever since. He comes and goes between trips."

"Did you know he's thinking about selling the ranch?" Cammie wanted to see if she got a reaction.

Ainsley's head shot up, her expression alarmed. "He wouldn't do that."

"I don't know. He showed it to somebody last week. He told me so. I assumed he might settle in Australia permanently."

"But he loves that ranch."

"That's what I said."

The two of them sat there for a moment, not speaking. Cammie didn't know what thoughts were running through Ainsley's mind. But Cammie's were clear. If Drake really did sell the ranch, she would know her chances of ending up with him were gone.

If he had no more ties to this town, he would have no reason to stay. With Ainsley an adult now, Drake could reclaim his life.

Pumpkin began to fuss.

Ainsley let him suck on her finger. "Can I go with you to change him? And could I give him his bottle?"

"That's dangerous, you know."

"What do you mean?" Ainsley's eyes widened.

"Soon you'll be as attached to him as I am, and then we'll both go to pieces when he leaves."

"I'll take that chance," Ainsley said, looking down at the baby with a soft smile. "Isn't it better to have loved and lost and all that?"

Cammie wasn't sure the sentiment was true. She remembered what it was like to lose Drake. Now, soon, she would have to go through the pain all over again.

Her life would have been far easier if she had never met him.

In the guest room, she and Ainsley laughed and played with the little boy as they got him ready for his nap and his feeding. Pumpkin was more animated now.

Cammie watched with a smile as Ainsley settled in the rocker. "He changes every day," she said. "I can already see his personality."

Ainsley rocked slowly and held the bottle at the correct angle. "I feel so bad for his parents. They must be grief-stricken. Even if they abandoned him on purpose, because they couldn't care for him, that must have been agonizing."

"I know." Cammie stretched out on the bed, content to watch Drake's beautiful and capable stepsister feed the baby. Her eyes drifted shut again.

That was a mistake. Even though she hadn't been in *this* bed last night with Drake, the memories of the moments they had shared in his room played behind her eyelids in vivid color. His big, masculine hands stroking her skin. The way his tousled hair made him look more carefree. The glint of heated sexual intent when he smiled at her.

She missed him already. It had only been a few hours, and she *missed him already*. How needy and self-destructive was that?

Once again, she thought about her options. What would he say if she offered to postpone her baby plans and come to Australia with him? He had actually suggested that very thing early on. Surely he hadn't changed his mind.

Of course, she couldn't leave with him tomorrow. She had responsibilities to the foundation and to her father and to all the men and women who would benefit from the announcement at the gala.

And honestly, if Drake went back to Sydney alone, what were the chances Cammie would really follow him? Wasn't it more likely that the connection would simply fade away? Their current sexual relationship was one of convenience. It probably wouldn't survive a separation.

Still, the thought of cutting all ties was impossible to contemplate.

Unfortunately, as good as Pumpkin had been all morning, he was now extremely fussy. Maybe he was overly tired. Ainsley walked him first, then Cammie. The baby fell asleep again and again but jerked awake if he was moved.

Finally, at almost one o'clock, he gave up the fight. Cammie laid him in the crib and held her breath. Ainsley approached the bed cautiously. "Is he out?" she whispered.

"I think so."

The tiptoed toward the door. Cammie grabbed the monitor. In the kitchen, both of them exhaled in relief.

Ainsley immediately started rummaging

in the refrigerator. "I'm starving," she said, pulling out leftover roast beef and opening a loaf of bread.

"Leave out a couple of slices for me, too," Cammie said. Ainsley was a very comfortable person to be around. Cammie liked her immensely. Maybe, even with Drake gone, the two women could be closer friends.

Cammie had known Drake's stepsister back when Cammie and Drake were dating, but not well.

When they finally sat down to their meal, Ainsley shot Cammie a sideways glance. "So do you really not have a thing for Drake anymore?"

"Does it matter?" Cammie asked wryly.

"I think it does. Maybe you could persuade him to come home for good. I know he's having a good time in Australia, but when you're born and bred in Royal, it sticks with you. I can't imagine him turning his back on his heritage."

"I told you. He's probably selling the ranch."

"Maybe. But even so, this is his town. It's part of his DNA. Wouldn't it be fun if the two of you passed that DNA on to another generation?"

"You're dreaming," Cammie said. "You admitted it. Taking care of you in your *difficult* years cured him of any desire for fatherhood."

"True." Ainsley took a sip of her soft drink and wrinkled her nose. "But I think he hangs on to that just to keep women from getting close to him."

"I *was* close to him," Cammie said bluntly. "And he broke up with me when he found out I wanted kids."

"Ouch." Ainsley seemed abashed. "I just assumed the two of you drifted apart."

"Nope. Your sainted stepbrother cut me loose. The thought of having a baby with me scared him spitless."

Twelve

Drake stood just outside the kitchen door, unashamedly eavesdropping. He hadn't eaten lunch yet. He could have joined the two women. But the thought of food made him ill. To hear Cammie put reality into words so succinctly twisted the knot in his stomach even tighter.

She was right. He *had* been scared. It wasn't so much that he didn't want to have kids. The truth was, he was *scared* to have kids. He had spent many sleepless nights over the last seven years wondering if he was screwing up his stepsister's life.

That uncertainty had dogged him at every

turn. For a man who was confident and focused in every other aspect of his life, his rocky relationship with his stepsister had pained him. He felt like their difficulties were entirely his fault.

How could he go through that again with a baby? What did he know about raising children? They weren't like horses and cows. A son or a daughter needed more than food and water. A child needed love and nurturing and attention.

Drake was pretty sure he was a failure at all those.

Finally, when enough time had passed and the conversation in the kitchen turned to innocuous topics, he walked into the room.

Even though his stepsister and his lover had been talking about a television show and nothing more intimate, they both looked guilty. Had they guessed he'd been in the hall for some time?

Drake pasted a carefree smile on his face. "Any news about Pumpkin?"

Cammie blushed, as though she couldn't look at him without remembering last night. "No," she said. "Haley Lopez promised to keep me in the loop, but apparently there's nothing to tell."

"You want a sandwich?" Ainsley asked.

He ruffled the ends of her hair. "No, thanks." He reached in the fridge for a bottle of water. "What about Sierra Morgan? Have we heard anything else from her?"

Again, Cammie shook her head. "She really wanted to do a follow-up story, but there's the same problem—no new information."

"I don't get it," Ainsley said. "What about security cameras and all that *NCIS* stuff? How did *no one* see what happened?"

"It was the middle of a huge parking lot," Drake said, sitting down across from Cammie and adjacent to his stepsister. "Whoever did this was careful not to get caught."

He could see that the conversation was bothering Cammie, so he changed the subject. "Ains," he said. "I need to talk to you about something important. Why don't we go to my office?"

His hideaway was a small room on the back of the house. He rarely used it anymore, but it was outfitted with all the necessary tech gadgets.

Ainsley gave him on odd stare. "I have no secrets from Cammie," she said.

Drake frowned, feeling as if the two women in his life were ganging up on him. "Maybe I do," he said.

Cammie jumped to her feet. "I'll leave you two alone. You have things to discuss."

Drake grabbed her wrist. "Good grief. Sit down. I was kidding. If Ainsley doesn't care, then I don't."

"Stay, Cammie," Ainsley said. "I might need reinforcements."

"You're making a big deal about nothing," Drake said. "All I wanted was to get your opinion about selling the ranch."

Both women were silent. Tight-lipped.

Finally, Ainsley sighed. "It's your property. I don't have a say."

"Is that true?" Now Cammie glared at him as if he was throwing Ainsley out on the street.

"Technically, yes," he said. "My father never changed his will before he died. Not intentionally, I'm sure. He was always busy, and financial details weren't his priority. But as it happens, everything came to me at their deaths. I've made sure that half of it is Ainsley's, of course."

His stepsister batted her eyes at him. "My hero." She made a face as she spoke to Cammie. "Why should I inherit a ranch that's been in the Rhodes family for generations? My mom was only married to Drake's dad for a year. I'm fine."

Then she looked back at Drake. "Seriously. It's your decision."

"But?" He lifted an eyebrow."

Cammie frowned. "Why is there a *but*?"

Drake saw the shadows under her eyes. He should feel bad for putting them there, but he was having a hard time concentrating on anything but the memory of Cam's naked body. That was the sole reason he had asked to speak to Ainsley in private.

He laughed. "There's always a *but* with Ainsley. She has opinions about everything. Many opinions."

"You're mean," Ainsley pouted.

"But you're not denying it. Go ahead," he said. "Speak your piece."

Ainsley stood and went to lean against the sink, facing Drake and Cammie. She crossed her arms, looking fierce. "Selling would be a mistake. I don't know if you're having some kind of midlife crisis, but this is dumb, Drake."

"I'm not even thirty," he protested.

Cammie snickered.

Ainsley went on. "You've always loved the ranch. And I'm pretty sure you regretted buying this house when we could have both been living there."

Drake leaned his chair back on two legs. "Maybe that's true. But things have changed. I've changed."

It surprised him when Cammie spoke. Her gaze seemed to see through his walls. "How?" she asked. "How have you changed? You're still closed off and a loner. Neither your stepsister nor I know what you're thinking most of the time."

Drake flinched, feeling the need to defend himself but not knowing what to say. An uncomfortable silence reigned in the kitchen.

Ainsley straightened. "I'm still not feeling a hundred percent," she said. "I think I'll go rest and read a magazine. Besides, if you're flying out tomorrow, Drake, I'm sure you and Cammie have things to talk about."

When his stepsister disappeared into the hall and up the stairs, they could hear her footsteps on the floor overhead. Drake exhaled. "She's right. We do need to talk."

Cammie fair skin paled even more. "About what?" She jumped up and began tidying the kitchen, as if she couldn't stand to be too close to him.

He shook his head slowly. "You. Me. Last night."

Now, two streaks of color high on her cheekbones proclaimed that she was either upset or embarrassed or both. "It was good," she said, the words flat.

"Good enough for a repeat tonight?" He wasn't expecting anything of the kind, but he wanted to see what she would say.

Cammie stopped what she was doing and stared at him. "I saw the printout of the flight info you gave Ainsley," she said. "You have to leave the house at 4:00 a.m. I don't think you have time for fooling around."

"I wonder why they call it that?" he said. "Makes it sound unimportant."

"Maybe the word you're looking for is *casual*...or *fun*."

He stood and took two steps in her direction. Cammie backed up against the refrigerator. Her hands were shoved in the pockets of her faded jeans. She looked young and innocent and incredibly appealing.

It was time for the question he had dreaded. But he couldn't move forward until he knew the truth. "Cam?"

He saw her throat move as she swallowed. "Yes?"

"Can I ask you something about your baby plans?"

A frown line appeared between her eyebrows. "I suppose."

"Why artificial insemination? Why not adopt?"

His question surprised her. He could tell.

She rubbed her forehead as if their sleepless night had given her a headache. "Well, I always hoped I would have more than one child. And I like the idea of adopting a boy or girl who might be a little older...maybe even seven or eight. You know...someone who has been overlooked."

"That doesn't really answer my question," he said. "Why artificial insemination?"

Cammie shrugged, her expression hard to read. "I want to be pregnant," she said. "I want to carry a baby."

Drake shouldn't be surprised. Not really. But could he live with the idea that another man's seed had created a child in Cammie's womb? His feelings were Neanderthal, most likely. But they were his feelings, and he didn't know what to do with them.

"I understand," he said. And he did. The image of Cammie with a rounded belly and a maternal glow tugged at a sore place in his heart.

Perhaps she wanted to change the subject, or maybe it was just his day for being shocked out of his complacency.

She actually relaxed her wary stance and came to him, sliding her arms around his waist and resting her cheek over his heart. "There's something I've wanted to ask *you*," she said, her voice soft and filled with feminine secrets.

"Oh?" He held her close, feeling his body's inevitable reaction, but concentrating on her words. He couldn't see her face in this position.

Cammie sighed. "You've made me curious about Australia. I'm tied down until after the gala, but what would you think if I came to visit you in Sydney?"

Cammie was so close to Drake there was no way she could miss the way his body stiffened.

He cleared his throat. "Um…"

Her heart shriveled. She'd thought he would be excited. Instead, she felt his shock and something else…dismay?

In a moment of blinding hurt, she jerked away from him. *"It was your idea,"* she said, tears burning her eyes. "But I get it. It's fine to screw around while you're in town. But me following you is not so appealing anymore. You've scratched the itch."

"No, Cammie…"

He held out a hand to touch her, but she slapped it away, a huge sob building in her chest. "I'm so stupid. I keep expecting you to change, but you're the same man who broke up with me two years ago. Go to hell, Drake.

Or to Australia. I don't care. But this time, do me a favor. Don't come back."

Cammie fled down the hall toward the back of the house and out into the sun-warmed yard. All around her, autumn frolicked. The day was beautiful, blue-skied and warm. The trees bent in the breeze. Texas was bright and verdant. But her world lay in ashes.

Somewhere deep in her silly, daydreaming heart, she had expected Drake to follow her. When he didn't, the tears came hard and fast. She was so tired of wanting things beyond her reach.

Her brother wouldn't come home despite her repeated pleas. Her father only cared about her organizational skills. Her mother was…well, who knew? Mostly a stranger now. And then there was Pumpkin, who despite everything Cammie had done for him would soon be going away.

What was wrong with her? Why did she offer up her heart only to let it be bruised and battered? Why did she let Drake drag her into his orbit again only to reject her even now when she thought they had been growing closer?

Unfortunately, she didn't have the luxury of wallowing in her self-pity. The baby monitor was still in the kitchen.

She dried her face on the hem of her shirt and marched back inside. Puffy eyes were impossible to conceal, but she had little pride left.

The kitchen was empty, as was the living room. She saw no trace of Drake but found Ainsley in the guest room feeding Pumpkin.

Ainsley's glance was sympathetic, almost more than Cammie could bear. "Drake asked me to look after the baby. He said you needed a moment alone."

"And is he still here?"

Ainsley shook her head slowly. "No. He took his keys and wallet and left."

"To go where?"

"I have no idea," Ainsley said. "I'm so sorry, Cammie. I know he must have hurt you some-how."

Cammie sat down on the edge of the bed. "It's my own fault. I keep expecting him to be someone he's not. And yet I keep coming back for more."

"Are you okay?"

"I will be. I just wish they would find Pumpkin's parents so I could get out of this house." She thumped the nearest pillow with her fist. "I want to go home."

Ainsley shook her head slowly. "No, you don't. Not really. You want to keep this sweet little boy."

"But we both know I can't. Love sucks."

"Now you're just being crazy."

Ainsley's droll comment made Cammie laugh in spite of her mood. "Thanks for covering for me."

"Well, we're a team now. When Drake leaves tomorrow, it will be just you and me taking care of this little sweetie."

Cammie flinched. "So, he's still going?"

"As far as I know."

It was bad enough that Drake was leaving. But to know he no longer cared enough to extend their relationship beyond today was a pain Cammie couldn't shake.

She stood and paced. "How are you feeling? Do your incisions hurt?"

"I'm better every day," Ainsley said. "Are you being nice, or is there a point to your questions?"

Busted. Cammie lifted her shoulders and let them fall, taking a deep breath in the process. She wouldn't let Drake destroy her a second time. "I desperately need to get a dress for the Cattleman's Club gala, and I'm running out of time. Do you think you could handle solo babysitting for a couple of hours?"

"Of course." Ainsley beamed. "This little fella and I will be fine. Go do what you want to do. Take your time."

Cammie changed clothes rapidly and gathered what she would need for her outing. She wanted to go by her place and check on things, but her home was in the opposite direction. That would have to wait for another day.

It wasn't fair to Ainsley to abandon her for very long.

Cammie made two brief stops and finally ended up at a high-end ladies' clothing store that concentrated on bridal and special occasion gowns. Fortunately for Cammie—probably because it was the middle of the afternoon on a weekday—the shop was empty. The single employee greeted her new customer warmly and jumped into action, gathering stacks of dresses for Cammie to try.

After the first dozen, Cammie was discouraged. She put on her own clothes again and came out of the fitting room. "So far I'm zero for twelve."

"Not to worry. We have plenty more."

With Cammie's red hair, some colors didn't work at all. One dress caught her eye because it was a little out of the ordinary. It was a deep forest green, fashioned close to the body and skimming her hips to the floor. Spaghetti straps supported a low-cut bodice. All over the delicate fabric, tiny, sparkly beads shimmered.

"I like this one," Cammie said. "I'll try it on next. Unless you think it's too fancy for the upcoming gala."

"Not at all," the woman said. "Everybody wants a reason to dress up these days. I've sold dozens of eye-catching gowns. And I think this one is probably going to be perfect on you."

Cammie stepped behind the curtain. The cut of the dress would make a bra impossible to hide. The bodice was lined and stiffened with boning. After stripping down to her undies…again…she slipped the beautiful garment over her head and reached behind, managing to get the zipper up.

The woman who looked back from the gilt-framed, floor-length mirror was almost a stranger. Cammie scooped her hair in one hand and held it on top of her head. Maybe she would try an updo for the night at the Cattleman's Club gala.

The dress was definitely flattering.

But she wouldn't mind a second opinion just to be sure. She pushed the curtain aside and stepped out onto the small platform. "What do you think of this one?"

Everything in the room spun when she saw not the saleslady, but Drake Rhodes. He stood, tall and gorgeous, with his arms crossed over his chest. The store employee was nowhere to be seen.

Drake's expression was serious, his blue eyes closer to midnight than summer sky. In fact, he seemed stunned. "It's absolutely perfect," he said, the words gruff. "You look like a princess."

Cammie resisted the urge to cover her chest

with her hands. She had a lot of bare skin exposed. "How did you find me?" she asked.

"Ainsley told me you had gone shopping for a gala dress. Not too many places in town available to do that. Natalie Valentine's shop seemed like the best bet."

"Why?" Cammie asked. "Why are you here?" He hadn't followed her to the backyard when she ran away from him. Why now?

His face was all planes and angles. In his eyes she fancied she saw pain, but that didn't make any sense. His demeanor was grim.

"Will you go out to the ranch with me?" he asked.

On any other day, she would have jumped at the chance. But now it hurt too much. She couldn't keep up the pretense that they were only friends with benefits. She loved the stubborn, frustrating man, and it was tearing her apart.

"I'm almost through here," Cammie said slowly. "But I've been gone too long. I have to get back to the house and relieve Ainsley."

"I've already talked to her," he said. "Mrs. Hampton is there now. The two of them are happy to care for the baby until you and I get back."

Cammie was at a loss. This didn't seem like a casual invitation. But on the other hand, what possible reason could Drake have for taking her to the ranch?

"I think I'll pass," she said. "But thanks anyway." She didn't say *maybe another time.* If Drake was selling the ranch, she would never see it again. That thought was both sad and painful.

She took a step backward, preparing to disappear into the fitting room.

Drake scowled. "Stop, Cam. I know I handled our last conversation badly. I'm sorry about that. You took me by surprise. I didn't—"

Cammie held up her hand. "No, no, no, Drake." She halted the words tumbling from his gorgeous lips. "I'm the one who should apologize. In the past, I've accused you of being inflexible, but maybe *I'm* the one who needs to bend occasionally. If I truly care about you, and I do, then I need to think about abandoning a few of my non-negotiables. That's why I mentioned Australia. I thought on neutral ground we might find a way to…" *To what?* She didn't know how to end that sentence, so she left it hanging.

Her explanation didn't seem to make things better. In fact, Drake was more grim-faced than ever.

"Cam…" He held out both hands. "Please. I have things to say, and we need somewhere with no interruptions."

What was left to *say*? He was leaving Royal tomorrow. Clearly, he had no interest in her following him to Australia. Still, curiosity was a powerful emotion. That, and the desire to spend a few more precious hours with the man she loved.

"Okay," she said, giving in mostly because she wanted to… "Let me pay for the dress, and I'll meet you outside."

His gaze narrowed. "I'll wait right here. You might duck out the back door."

She turned on her heel and flounced away. Unfortunately, the space she had to cover was three steps at most, so it was hard to make a dramatic retreat.

The dressing cubicle didn't actually have a door that closed. The only barrier between her and Drake was a pair of heavy damask drapes striped in gold and burgundy. Normally, they were tied back with ornate cords. When closed, anyone who really wanted to might peek through the tiny gaps.

Cammie stripped off the gown, laying it with care across the satin-covered chair. She dressed rapidly, feeling as though Drake might have X-ray vision. Her nipples pebbled at the thought. He was so close and yet so far away.

When she was presentable, she ran a brush through her hair and touched up her lip gloss. Finally, she couldn't delay any longer. As she shoved back the curtains and exited the small area, she saw that Drake had sprawled in one of the comfy chairs designated for spouses or other waiting guests.

He rolled to his feet when Cammie came out. She wondered if he noticed the transformation from prom queen to tomboy. Her clothing—old jeans and a very casual cream-colored sweater—was not what she would have chosen to wear for a heart-to-heart with her lover. Already, she felt at a disadvantage.

Still, why did it matter what she was wearing? Drake had seen her naked, had made love to her again and again. If his regard for her was no more than physical, clothes were the least of her worries.

Thirteen

Drake drove in the general direction of the ranch, winding through town, taking his time before getting out into the countryside. He should have been working his game plan, gently moving the conversation in the direction he wanted it to go.

But all he could concentrate on was how Cammie had looked in that dark emerald dress. Vibrant, sexy. Utterly desirable in every way. He had wanted to take her just like that…to lift her skirts and tumble her over the arm of a chair. The urge had been so powerful, he'd actually felt sweat bead his forehead.

Now, to keep his hands from trembling, he gripped the steering wheel.

He drove on autopilot. The air inside the car was heavy and silent, crushed perhaps by the weight of the deep, arctic crevasse between them. Cammie didn't want to be here, that was for certain.

The ranch gates were not open this time. It was late in the afternoon. The day laborers would have gone home. His on-site guys would be in the bunkhouse having a beer and getting ready for dinner.

Drake put the car in Park, opened the gate, moved the car and closed the gate. The metal bars were heavy and hard to manage. Cammie didn't offer to help, nor did he ask.

He took the same route he had followed earlier. Only this time, he stopped at the house. Cammie got out and stared at the two-story Texas home where Drake had been reared. There had been spankings aplenty, but he had never doubted that he was loved.

She had her arms wrapped tightly around her as if she was cold. But even with the sun going down, the air was mild. He suspected her unconscious posture was protective.

He faced her across the top of the car. "I'd like to go for a ride. Together. On one horse. Is that okay with you?"

"Sure." She shrugged. There was little enthusiasm in the word.

Instead of going inside, he walked around the house toward the barn. Cammie followed him. Drake had called ahead and asked one of the wranglers to put the big saddle on Drake's favorite stallion.

The horse was waiting, raring to go. He lifted his head and whinnied when Drake approached the stall. "Hey there, old boy. Ready to stretch your legs?"

Fortunately, the vigorous animal was far more excited about the plan than Drake's human guest.

Cammie wrinkled her nose. "Isn't this Diablo?"

Drake checked the cinch automatically. "Yep. But he's older now. He'll behave." He glanced over his shoulder. "Front or back?"

This time, the wrinkle in her brow threatened to become permanent. "Front, I guess. I want to see where I'm going." She pulled an elastic band from her pocket and secured her hair low on the back of her neck.

"Fair enough." Drake swung into the saddle and reached down. "Grab my hand."

In the past, they had done this dozens of times. Cammie remembered the routine. She let him pull her up easily. When she settled between his arms, he picked up the reins. "Here we go."

It was dangerous to ride in the dark. Drake's plan was smashed up against the need to keep Cammie safe. He had a limited amount of daylight.

Because of that, he let Diablo have his head, going from a trot in the barnyard to a flat-out gallop when they exited the fence. Cammie was forced into Drake's chest whether she wanted to be or not.

He inhaled her scent, losing himself in the mad dash, wanting to ride forever with the woman he loved in his embrace. But there were things to be said. When they approached the tree where he had done his heavy thinking earlier in the day, Drake slowed the horse and stopped on top of the rise.

He wound the reins over the lowest branch, helped Cammie down and walked her to the far side of the hill that faced the sunset. There was a stump and a rock. He gave her the stump and sat facing her.

Cammie focused her attention on the colors of the sky. If he had special ordered the moment, it couldn't have been any more perfect. Because his Cam seemed unable to look at him, he saw her in profile.

Strong chin. Cute nose. Smooth brow. Strands of hair that had escaped during their ride, dancing in the breeze.

With the moment now at hand, Drake found his voice frozen.

Cammie turned her head. "Why are we here, Drake?"

He swallowed. "I need your opinion."

"On what?"

"On whether or not to sell the ranch."

That cute but aggravating frown was back. "Why ask me? I'm no finance whiz."

He stood at the edge of forever and saw both ways this could go. "Because I love you," he said gruffly.

* * *

Cammie was stunned. And not at all sure she had heard him correctly. For a man who had just professed love to a woman, he looked remarkably miserable.

"We'll circle back to that last bit," she said, refusing to believe him. "Again, I'll ask, why my opinion? Either you want to keep this place, or you don't."

Perhaps she wasn't being very diplomatic, but she was confused. And afraid.

Drake leaned forward, resting his hands on his knees. "When we were dating, did you ever visualize the two of us living here together?"

"Um…" That was a tough one. But he was looking at her so intently, she had to answer truthfully. "We were *dating*," she said. "It was casual."

He refused to be put off. "A year and a half isn't casual. We might not have made any firm plans, but we were more than casual. Surely you thought about it."

"Fine," she said, giving in to his inquisition. "Yes. Once in a while. I did think about it. I could see the two of us growing old here."

"Why did you never say anything?"

"Good grief, Drake. A woman can't wear her heart on her sleeve. And certainly not with a man like you."

He raised an eyebrow. "A man like me?"

"You were a complicated puzzle in almost every way. I knew you enjoyed the sex, but beyond that, I had no clue what you were thinking. Needless to say, when we finally shared our dreams for the future, it became crystal clear that your bucket list and mine weren't even written in the same language. And then when you dumped me, it was so gradual at first, I didn't see the end coming."

His expression grew darker still. "I made a mistake," he said. "A bad one. I hurt you. I'm sorry, Cammie."

She shook her head slowly, trying to sift through his words. "It wasn't your fault," she said. "You were trying to do the right thing in a bad situation."

"But I made it worse. I didn't know until you were gone how much you meant to me. That's trite, I know, but it's true."

Because I love you. His words echoed in her head. She honestly wondered if she had dreamed them. She did have an overactive imagination. "Drake…" She shook her head slowly. "I don't know what this is about, but it doesn't make sense. We ran into each other purely by chance at the hospital. You were racing home to see Ainsley, who was seriously ill. You said it yourself…reuniting with me wasn't at the top of your list."

He scowled. "You told me I was complicated. Maybe I am. And maybe I'm stupid, too. About women, at least. The subconscious is a powerful beast."

"People don't change overnight. *You* don't change overnight. I get that you're conflicted about selling the ranch, but that has nothing to do with me."

His hands fisted on his knees. She could almost see the control he was fighting to keep. "I told you why. I love you."

He was saying words she had longed to hear, but he was so obviously tormented, she couldn't in good conscience take him at his word. "I offered to visit you in Australia. To see if there was some middle ground we could find. You practically threw your back out avoiding that idea. I don't understand you."

"I don't understand myself," he muttered. "I've been thinking about the baby thing…a lot. Maybe it wouldn't be so bad."

Cammie leaped to her feet, suddenly unable to continue this conversation. It was tearing her apart. "May we go?" she asked with little finesse. "I'm getting cold."

That wasn't entirely true, but this wind-blown sunset moment was too beautiful and not beautiful enough. Even if she could believe his words, one of them was going to have to choose. If either was wrong, the relationship was doomed.

Drake rose and untied the horse, not saying a word. The trip back was far slower. Dark piled up quickly when the sun slipped behind the horizon. For the last quarter mile, the horse had to pick his way cautiously.

In the barn, Cammie hopped down. "You'll have to take care of the horse, right?"

Drake shook his head. "No. One of my men is on standby. As soon as I text him, he'll come."

They walked toward the house, close but not touching.

Drake unlocked the door and turned on a light. Someone had laid logs and kindling in the fireplace. With one match, the fire blazed.

Cammie pulled up a small rocker and stared into the flames. Her stomach growled audibly.

Finally, Drake chuckled. "Stay there and get warm. I'll bring the food."

"You don't need help?"

"Nope."

Five minutes later he returned bearing a platter of turkey sandwiches, two water bottles and a bag of chips. "It's a far cry from the Bellamy, but it was all I could arrange on short notice."

"It looks good." Cammie wasn't going to complain. She had only eaten a sandwich for lunch, and it was late now.

Drake pulled up the chair that matched hers. Their knees were almost touching as they wolfed down the simple meal.

"We should get back," Cammie said abruptly. "I need to check on the baby."

"I just texted Ainsley. Everything is fine."

He wiped his mouth with a napkin and stared at her.

"What?" Cammie said. "Do I have mayonnaise on my chin?"

Drake took her plate, stacked it with his and set both on the hearth. Then he leaned back in his seat, his big frame dwarfing the small rocker, and sighed. "When a man tells a woman he loves her, he usually expects some kind of answer."

"Oh." Cammie felt woozy. "You were serious?"

"Of course I was serious. Why would I say it if I didn't mean it?"

The look of indignation on his face almost made her laugh. But the situation was far too serious and fraught with pitfalls. "You've been under a lot of stress," she muttered. "Sometimes people crack."

His jaw went granite hard. Those blue eyes that were her downfall pinned her with a laser gaze. "Do you want to tell *me* something, Cam?"

"Like what?" Anxiety threatened to overwhelm her.

"Do you love me?"

There was so much tenderness in his words, she felt tears burn her eyes. "Of course I love you." She couldn't look at him. "Don't be dumb. Why else would I let you crook your finger and I'd come running after two years apart? A woman doesn't do that just because you're good in bed."

"I see."

When she sneaked a look at him, his lips were twitching. "Don't laugh at me, Drake," she said. "This is serious. I would give up having kids to be with you. I *would*. But what if I get mean and bitchy down the road and start to resent you and ruin our marriage? Adoption wouldn't be much better from your standpoint. We could find an older child so we could skip over the baby years, but Ainsley wasn't even a baby. She was *fifteen*, and look how that turned out."

He scooped her out of her chair and carried her to the comfy sofa nearby. "Did I propose?" he asked. "I must have missed that part." The huge piece of furniture was upholstered in a soft, crinkly velvet that felt both authentic to the house and yet extremely comfortable. The rust-colored fabric echoed the colors in the fire.

When Drake snuggled her close, she felt how fast his heart was beating. And he definitely had a boner. Somehow, that made her feel better.

When he stroked her hair, she felt like crying.

"I want to have babies with you Cammie," he said, his voice gruff with emotion. "I swear I do. And it doesn't matter to me if we adopt or go another route. The important thing is that you believe me. I'm not saying this just to get what I want."

"What *do* you want?" she asked, her words tremulous.

"You," he said simply. "And a family. I've been a selfish, stubborn idiot. I almost lost you because I was so blind. I don't know why I clung to that no-baby thing for so long. I've given it a lot of thought lately, and maybe it was because I was scared, scared I couldn't be a good dad. I'm not used to failing all that often, but being a parent is so much harder than succeeding at business. I think I didn't want to admit how helpless I felt, how uncertain and unqualified. I was afraid to take a chance. But now I realize. You and I together can do *anything*. A baby is a miracle. Little Pumpkin has reminded me of that. And all the trauma with Ainsley was worth it because of the relationship it forged. She and I are solid."

Suddenly, Cammie's pocket vibrated. She wriggled sideways, pulled out her cell and looked at the screen. It was Haley Lopez. After hours.

"Are you going to answer it?" Drake asked.

Cammie couldn't hit the button. "What if they've found Pumpkin's mother? What if they're taking him away tonight?"

She lost it then. From the moment she found a baby on her car and then saw Drake striding back into her life, her world had been turned upside down. Thinking Drake was leaving tomorrow had been the final straw.

She let the call go to voice mail because she was sobbing too hard to speak.

Drake let her cry it out, petting her and whispering sweet things in her ear. About how beautiful she was and how smart and how caring.

Eventually, she ran out of steam. "Sorry," she whispered. "I got your shirt all wet."

His arms tightened around her. "Marry me, Cam. Let's build a family together."

She laid her cheek over his heart. "Yes."

It was such an easy thing to say. Drake jerked when he heard it, as if she had struck him somehow. Surely he wasn't surprised by her answer. Not after this week.

Even so, she felt the tension in him.

"But there's something I have to tell you," he said.

There was an odd note in his voice. Because she was anxious again, she let her words flow, unfiltered. "What? You have another fiancée in Australia? You're not really rich? Or maybe you already have some kids tucked away I don't know about?"

He shifted her so she was sitting beside him. The expression on his face was sober. "Before you commit to a lifetime with me, darlin', you should know. I may not be *able* to get you pregnant."

"Why? What do you mean?" She searched his face to see if he was kidding.

But Drake wasn't joking. "I was snorkeling

near Melbourne and got careless. Cut my leg on some coral. Didn't go to the doctor right away. Let the wound get infected. By the time I went in to get it looked at, they were concerned about flesh-eating bacteria."

Her eyes widened. "That's not an urban legend?"

He choked out a laugh. "No. It's a real thing. They put me on steroids and almost a month of a high-powered antibiotic. The doctor this morning told me it can cause male sterility."

"*Can?* But not for sure?"

"He suggested that before I start trying for a child with my partner, I should consult a specialist."

In a sudden burst of clarity, Cammie saw her whole future. "That's fine," she said, unbuttoning his shirt and stroking his collarbone. "Sounds like a challenge to me."

"Cammie?" His voice was strained. "What are you doing?"

"I just got engaged. That calls for celebration sex." She kissed him with all she was feeling, exulting inwardly when his arms came around her and dragged her against his chest.

He kissed her right back. And then some. Suddenly the room was *too* warm.

Drake began stripping her out of her clothes, even as she clumsily tried to help him. Both of them gave up halfway through. He eased her onto her back, his eyes dark with arousal. "I didn't bring any protection."

Cammie rubbed her thumb over his bottom lip. "I don't care if you don't."

Heat flared in his gaze. "This is so damn sexy," he growled.

As he freed his erection and moved between her thighs, she smiled. "Trying to make a baby?"

"No. Making love to my gorgeous fiancée." He thrust deep, forcing a keening cry from her throat.

She wrapped her legs around his back. "I haven't seen a ring yet," she panted. "So it's not entirely official."

"Feels pretty damn official to me."

They were hungry for each other. It had been hours since he touched her like this. Cammie came before he did, crying out. This time was different, though. She felt hope and joy and a blinding certainty that they were going to make it.

When Drake climaxed moments later, his big body rigid and hot above hers, she buried her face in his shoulder.

Wow. She stroked his back, or the part she could reach. His shirt was shoved up to his armpits. Her sweater was in the same shape.

She started to laugh. She couldn't help it.

Drake sat up finally, his expression priceless. "Not the reaction I was hoping for, my Cam."

"Look at us," she said.

When he did, a sheepish wince was his only response.

She straightened her clothes and stood up. "I guess I should listen to the voice message from Haley."

Drake took care of his own attire and yawned. "She's probably working the late shift and is just checking in."

"I hope that's all it is." Cammie's heartbeat skittered as she pressed the button and listened. Relief flooded her as she processed the message. "They haven't found Pumpkin's family yet," she said, looking at Drake with tears in her eyes. "But because the situation is dragging on, the social services lady needs to do another home visit."

"See," Drake said. "Crisis averted."

He took her wrist and reeled her in, kissing her lazily, pointing out without words that the hum of excitement between them was only momentarily banked. "Besides," he said. "You're a tough woman. You've known all along that the day will come when you have to give Pumpkin back. You'll be fine, I promise. I'll be right there beside you when we hand him over. I love you, Cammie. And I'll love our babies, however we have them. I'm sorry it took me so long to realize that I was being an ass."

"I was part of the problem," she insisted. "I was so fixated on getting pregnant, I couldn't admit that I loved you more than I wanted my dream. *You* are my dream," she said. "Babies or no babies. If I have you, I'll be happy."

"Take off your clothes," he said, his expression droll.

"Excuse me?" She lifted an eyebrow.

"Isn't this the occasion for makeup sex?"

"Goofy man. Let's go home to your wonderful bed." She paused, staring up at him with a teasing smile. "And my answer is no."

Shock flashed across his face. "No what?"

"No. Don't you dare sell this ranch."

He cupped her cheeks in his hands and kissed her until her toes curled. "Don't worry, Cam. I've got a very good imagination. I'm already thinking about all the ways I'm going to screw you in this house."

"And in the barn. And out under the stars. And—"

He put a hand over her mouth. "Don't tempt me, Camellia." He banked the fire and poured water on it.

Then they walked out to the car. A million stars shone overhead.

Cammie sighed. Had there ever been a more perfect night? Suddenly, she froze, her hand on the car door. "But what about your plane ticket tomorrow and the gala? We didn't figure out what to do."

He tucked her in and joined her in the car, leaning over to kiss her one last time before he started the engine. His smile was a flash of white in the semidarkness. "We covered the important stuff, my love. The rest will work itself out."

* * * * *